Mystery
of the
Emerald
Buddha

Mystery of the Emerald Buddha

BY BETTY CAVANNA

William Morrow and Company
New York 1976

Library of Congress Cataloging in Publication Data

Cavanna, Betty (date)
    Mystery of the Emerald Buddha.

SUMMARY: When the sacred Emerald Buddha is stolen from a Bangkok temple, a young girl and her father try to solve the mystery surrounding its disappearance.
    [1. Mystery and detective stories. 2. Thailand—Fiction]
I. Title.
PZ7.C286Mx7   [Fic]   76-21826
ISBN 0-688-22086-X
ISBN 0-688-32086-4 lib. bdg.

Mystery of the Emerald Buddha

¶1

Lisette sat erect on the edge of the leather chair in the publisher's office, her legs primly crossed at the ankles, her face expressionless, although her gray eyes secretly appraised the editor and the photographer seated on either side of the desk.

"How long do you think it will take, Alex? One

month? Two?" The thin, graying editor rested his elbows on the desk and twirled a pencil between his thumbs and forefingers. He was soft-spoken, but his manner was brisk and professional.

The younger man, bearded and blue-eyed, shrugged. "Depends on the weather. We'll be there during the rainy season, you know."

The editor nodded. "For the inside shots, that won't matter. For the exteriors the rains may even help."

"Help? How?"

"By washing the air." With a wry grin the editor indicated the cloudy window, beyond which Lisette could sense rather than see the feeble June sunshine touching the tall buildings rimming a canyonlike street that led, arrow straight, uptown, to the part of New York City where, unbelievably, she had been born.

"I understand there's smog in Bangkok, too," the editor was saying, as Lisette's glance strayed to the books crowding the shelves behind his head, then shifted to the virtual stranger who, nevertheless, was her father. The relationship seemed as improbable as her birthplace. Although she had spoken both English and French from the time she had learned to talk, Lisette didn't feel in the least American.

Nor did she look it. Slight, dark-haired, and pale,

she felt like a sparrow among a flock of blue jays when she walked on the city streets. And her clothes were as different as her appearance and her manners. In no time at all she had realized that to New Yorkers she was inescapably French.

The conversation between the two men was becoming more technical. "What format do you have in mind?" Alex asked his editor. "Can you give me the breakdown between color and black-and-white?" Pulling out a worn, pocket-sized notebook, Alex riffled through the pages to find an empty one. Meanwhile, the editor swung around in his chair and reached for a big art book with a glossy jacket.

"This is the sort of thing we're talking about," he explained as he handed it to Lisette.

The book was about Brazil, a country that to Lisette seemed as remote as Thailand. The volume was very handsome, very heavy, and very expensive, as she could see from the dollar price printed on the front jacket flap. Converted, it would add up to 140 French francs!

Skipping the descriptive blurb, her eyes settled on a line at the bottom of the flap: Photographs by Alexander Paul. Slowly she began to turn the pages, marveling that her own father had taken these pictures, that he had roamed the world on such assignments while, unknowing, Lisette had spent a quiet childhood in a remote French village in the district of Seine-et-Oise.

In all those years she had seen her father rarely. She could count on her fingers the infrequent times when her mother, in response to a telephone call, had bundled Lisette into the car and driven her to Paris to have lunch "with Papa, who is passing through."

Papa always brought her a present, a fuzzy animal, a doll, a book, a wristwatch. It was possible to date his visits roughly by recalling the increasing sophistication of the gifts. Yet the bearer became no more real to Lisette as she grew older. He appeared rather as a shadow from her mother's past, to be forgotten as soon as she returned to the familiar world of the manoir and the convent school.

Only her father's blue eyes, bright as the periwinkle hugging the manoir wall, had persisted in her memory from one year to another. Their expression was changeable, sometimes piercing, frequently laughing, occasionally questioning, but the color stayed as luminous as the Brazilian sky in the beautiful color photographs she was inspecting one by one.

They were remarkably youthful eyes, Lisette recognized, as she surreptitiously studied her father's eyes, so lively and full of anticipation that they made his bearded face look almost boyish. By comparison,

Lisette thought in passing, her aristocratic, modish mother seemed settled and mature.

She missed her mother. To avoid a stab of homesickness, Lisette closed the book and shifted it so that it could rest more evenly on her knees. Then her attention reverted to the conversation.

"Kyle Goodfellow, who's doing the text, is a curator from the Boston Museum," the editor was saying. "Kyle's over there already and has arranged to have you put up at one of the guesthouses reserved for foreign dignitaries. That's a bit of luck, because you'll be staying inside the palace grounds and able to take full advantage of the early morning and late afternoon light."

Palace? They were to live in a palace? Lisette, knowing only Versailles and Fontainebleau, visited on school excursions, tried to imagine what a palace in Bangkok might be like.

"You know, Alex," the editor continued, "the present king of Thailand was born in this country, in Cambridge, as a matter of fact, while his father was going to Harvard." His eyes twinkled. "The Boston connection may explain Kyle's success in getting you such posh accommodations."

Alex chuckled, then asked, "Do you expect the picture sequence to be firmed up by the time I arrive?"

13

"I should hope so," the editor said, then unexpectedly turned to Lisette. "And how are you going to spend the summer, young lady?"

Before she could reply her father broke in. "Oh, didn't I tell you? I'm taking Liz along." At the editor's expression of surprise, he added with a grin, "At my own expense, of course."

A frown, quickly controlled, creased the editor's forehead. "I don't know, Alex," he murmured. "Are you sure that's wise?"

"Why shouldn't it be?"

"Because this is a very demanding and time-consuming job," the editor replied quickly. To Lisette, he said, "I don't know what you'd find to do with yourself all day."

"I'll be all right," Lisette replied, displaying more confidence than she felt. Actually the thought of spending the rest of the summer in a Far Eastern country with this comparative stranger who happened to be her father made her heart flutter apprehensively. Homesickness struck again, with the force of a slap in the face. All other summers she had gone with Maman to Brittany, where she had always had playmates. Later they became companions, and out of the group emerged, last year, a boy named Philippe, her first real beau.

As though reading her thoughts, the editor remarked doubtfully, "There won't be any other young people around."

"I know," Lisette responded weakly, as she twisted her hands in her lap. Then, with an effort, she repeated, "I'll be all right."

"Of course you will!" Her father confirmed vigorously. "There will be plenty of things to do. We'll go sightseeing—"

"In the rain?" the editor questioned dryly.

"In the rain," said Alex. "We won't melt."

"No, but you'll steam unpleasantly," said the editor with a quirk of one eyebrow. "However, so be it, Alex. I can see you've made up your mind." He pushed back his chair, indicating clearly that the interview was nearing an end. There was some desultory talk about probable expenses for film and travel, mention of something called a drawing account, a bit of professional joking that Lisette couldn't follow. Then they were on their feet.

Ushered into a broad corridor leading to the elevators, Lisette preceded the two men, who lingered behind to exchange a final word in the doorway. A pretty red-haired secretary, seated at a desk in an alcove close to the office, looked up from her typewriter and smiled. "Hello," she said pleasantly.

"Hello," Lisette replied. Her attention was caught by the typewriter, a very up-to-date electric. She moved closer so that she could inspect it. "What a marvelous machine!"

The secretary nodded. "It does everything but talk."

"I learned to type last year in school," Lisette ventured. "It's a great convenience."

This remark seemed to amuse the secretary. She laughed as she replied, "It is that!"

The men caught up, and Alex introduced Lisette.

"Your *daughter!*" exclaimed the secretary. "I didn't know you had a daughter, Mr. Paul. You've certainly been keeping her a secret."

Alex seemed only slightly discomfited. "She lives with her mother in France," he explained briefly, then shook hands with his editor, and steered Lisette toward the elevator.

"Well, that's that," he murmured as they were whisked from the thirtieth to the first floor. "Now all I have to do is get the show on the road."

"Excusez?" Lisette was puzzled.

"It's just an expression," her father said without explaining. "It'll take you a while to get used to American slang."

I'll never get used to it, Lisette thought, but she didn't contradict him. In fact, during the ride uptown on a crowded Madison Avenue bus, she scarcely spoke at all.

16

Groaning and hissing, the bus seemed to be hurrying toward some dread disaster, carrying Lisette at the vortex of a swirl of people. Unfamiliar bodies, sharp-edged packages, bulging shopping bags pushing against her created a sense of panic. She wanted to scream.

The crush had separated her from her father, who seemed more of a stranger than ever as he stood hanging onto a strap and rocking lightly with the motion. A stranger among other strangers, Alexander Paul. And I am Lisette Paul, but I have no sense of belonging to him at all.

Subconsciously Lisette realized that this feeling was partly her mother's fault. She had overprotected her shy little daughter, raised her with an English nanny in a conventional French manner characteristic of a time gone by. Only recently had Lisette learned about the breakup of her parents' brief marriage, which had been more in the nature of a teen-age escapade than a serious commitment to matrimony.

At the time her father and mother had met in Washington, D.C., Alex was working at his first job with a daily newspaper. Invited in his professional capacity to a garden party at the French Embassy, he had met Julie Lassiat, whose father was in the United States on a Government mission. The attraction between the two was instant. Julie, very young and susceptible, on her first trip abroad, had been swept off her feet by the vitality of the American. They eloped to Maryland and were married. Julie remained behind when her parents were called back to France.

Lisette could not imagine the life of the young couple, whose backgrounds were so very different. She knew they had moved to New York, that she had been born a year later, and that before another year had passed her mother had carried her back to France, where she considered they both belonged.

And that's where I do belong, raged Lisette inwardly, as she clung to the bus strap, buffeted by the throng. Never in her life had she felt more alone.

"Hey, Liz!"

Lisette didn't react. Neither the voice nor the nickname had any impact.

"Hey, Liz!" A man's hand reached across the shoulders of a stout black woman and tugged at her sleeve. "Next stop."

The apartment was a haven of peace and quiet after the street. Although there was no view and little sunlight, it seemed like a nest to Lisette, littered with books and glossy photographs, masculine and untidy, but nevertheless snug and safe.

She kicked off her sandals and sank down on the

sofa gratefully. "I'd go crazy," she said, "if I had to live in New York."

"You sound like your mother."

Lisette nodded. "She must have hated it."

Alex shrugged out of his jacket and loosened his tie. "Or me."

"Oh, no, Papa! Maman always speaks kindly of you."

Alex grinned. He seemed in no need of this shred of consolation. "There's something about being called Papa—especially the way you pronounce it—that always gives me a start. It's so very formal, somehow, and so foreign. Couldn't you settle for Pop or Dad?"

Lisette thought for a minute, then said, rather haltingly, "I don't think so."

"How about Alex?"

Without hesitation Lisette shook her head. "That would not be proper. You *are* my father."

Laughing with honest amusement rather than embarrassment, Alex replied, "I *am* your father, Liz, but I wish we could get on a less formal basis, that's all."

"I see what you mean," said Lisette gravely. "You'd like me to give you a nickname."

"That's it."

"How about Papaul?"

Alex tried the word on his tongue. "Papaul. That's not bad."

And somehow it was easier for Lisette to say than Papa. It shortened the distance between them ever so slightly, because they had arrived at a solution together.

While Alex phoned his travel agent and a doctor who could give them the necessary innoculations, Lisette was drafted to fix lunch, which seemed to be a catch-as-catch-can affair here, rather than the main meal of the day, as it always was at the manoir. Americans apparently subsisted on sandwiches, especially one called a BLT, which consisted of tomato salad topped with bacon and eaten between two pieces of toast.

As she worked in the small kitchen, where no piece of equipment was more than an arm's length away, she could hear Alex talking about air schedules and possible routes. "See if you can book us on KLM to Amsterdam tomorrow night, then on to Bangkok via Vienna, Athens, and Karachi. That's faster than the Pacific jaunt. For two. No, not my wife, my daughter.

"Alexander Paul. P-a-u-l. That's the last name. And Miss Lisette Paul. L-i-s-e-t-t-e." There was a pause, a thank you, and the sound of the receiver rattling into its cradle.

Tomorrow night! So soon! Lisette paused with the sandwiches half made, dismayed, yet secretly intrigued by a sense of adventure. Her natural shyness was nearly smothered by a quality she didn't know that she possessed—curiosity.

The moment he finished his sandwich and the glass of beer he had poured, Alex picked up the telephone again and called his publisher's office. "One thing we overlooked," he mentioned to the editor. "Do you have any special thoughts on a jacket photo?"

The reply came through to Lisette only as a crackling on the wire. Then Alex said, "The Emerald Buddha. OK. We'll see what we can do."

He hung up and tugged at his beard. "The Emerald Buddha, huh?" He turned to Lisette. "The nuns ever teach you about the Emerald Buddha?"

Lisette shook her head. "I've never heard of him."

Alex chuckled. "Neither have I. But we'll find out who he is and where he lives soon enough!"

¶II

At two o'clock in the morning, Pakistan time, the plane put down in Karachi. Except for a few passengers disembarking, most of the travelers stayed in their seats. Alex, however, wanted to stretch his legs, so Lisette followed him down the steps and across the tarmac to a dingy terminal, where a sweaty barman in a soiled white coat was glumly wiping glasses with a rag.

"Want something cool to drink, Liz?"

Lisette looked at the rag in the barman's hand and shuddered. "No, thank you."

Alex ordered a beer. "Finicky, aren't you?" Although he didn't add, "Just like your mother," the words hovered in the stale, stifling air.

"I've never traveled much, outside of France," Lisette murmured as an excuse, then wondered why she had bothered. Her lip curled in instinctive distaste. The whole place looked filthy.

Correctly interpreting the expression, Alex laughed. "You learn to roll with the punches in my business," he said.

Another Americanism, Lisette thought. Rather descriptive, actually. She glanced around the terminal building in order to avoid looking at the barman. A trio of swarthy gentlemen—Pakistani, Indonesian, Indian?—were conferring solemnly in a corner; a child in the arms of a sari-clad young woman with a caste mark on her forehead was crying softly; and a few in-transit passengers were wandering to and fro like ghosts.

"You know," Alex said unexpectedly, "this trip may be just what the doctor ordered, Liz. You could use a little shaking up."

Lisette didn't reply because she didn't know what to say. She wished desperately that she were either back at the manoir in her own comfortable bed or in the more Spartan summer surroundings of Brittany—anywhere but here in this flyblown airport standing beside a man with rumpled hair, an open-throated sport shirt, which she considered more appropriate to tennis than to traveling, and a pair of dusty loafers with run-over heels. Americans didn't care how they dressed apparently. The English on board looked moderately respectable, but her father didn't even wear a tie.

Alex laughed again, a low, throaty chuckle. "You're a little ashamed of me, aren't you?" He set his empty beer mug back on the bar and without waiting for an answer said, "It'll take us a while to get to know each other, if we ever do."

Such offhand frankness was disturbing, even impolite. Trained by the nuns in courtesy, Lisette searched for a remark that would be reassuring. Nothing occurred to her, so she stifled a yawn, rubbed her eyes, and decided to climb back on board.

Once she was alone, indignation swept her. Alex could try a little harder to act like a parent, be a little more understanding, couldn't he? Instead, he had spent most of the trip strolling the aisles restlessly, stopping to chat here and there with anyone who caught his attention. Such nonchalance seemed brash to Lisette, such a free-and-easy manner beyond her comprehension.

The KLM stewardesses were busy folding rumpled blankets and gathering up abandoned newspapers, trying to bring order from the inevitable havoc wrought on each leg of the interminable flight. Once more settled in her seat, Lisette was only vaguely aware of their activity. Not until a man's voice boomed over the loudspeaker system did she become alert.

"Ladies and gentlemen, this is your captain speaking. I am sorry to have to announce a delay. The temperature control on number four engine is malfunctioning. Amsterdam has ordered us to remain here until a replacement arrives and can be installed. We are expecting to remain on the ground for about five hours."

A groan, carried on multiple voices, swept the airplane like a ground swell. Passengers—most of whom looked to Lisette like tired businessmen—got up, stretched, moved about, visited the lavatories, and ordered Bloody Marys. Drinks, the stewardesses explained, were on the house.

Lisette sighed. Then she retracted the armrest between her seat and her father's empty one, curled up like a kitten, and tried to go to sleep.

Dawn was breaking in the eastern sky when she awakened, and the stewardesses were passing out glasses of orange juice: plastic glasses, frozen juice, diluted to drinkable strength. Still, it was cold. Lisette accepted a glass gratefully and tried to smile as she said, *"Merci, mam'selle."*

"Vous en pris." The stewardess switched from one language to another automatically, while Lisette reverted to French only when she wasn't thinking. Although she was thoroughly at ease in English, her mother's tongue was more natural for her.

"Hi, Liz. Feeling better?"

Looking up into her father's face, Lisette considered. "I think so."

"Know how long you slept?"

"Two hours?"

"More like four. I came back twice, but you were dead to the world."

"Four hours! We should be leaving soon then."

"Don't count on it," advised Alex. "We may be spending the summer here. Want to step outside and test the climate again? It's like a steam bath."

Lisette shook her head, then abruptly changed her mind because she didn't want to seem petulant. "All right. Maybe I should walk around a bit."

In the terminal building, the same sweaty bartender was serving small cups of syrupy black coffee to an assortment of passengers who looked even more haggard in the morning light than they had at midnight. The men, by and large, were unshaven; the women had dark circles under their eyes.

One couple only seemed to have survived the long, uncomfortable night in a state approaching good grooming, and Alex led Lisette toward this stalwart pair. The woman was in her thirties, with hair that appeared artificially lightened and expensive clothes a size too small for her present build. Her companion, perhaps twenty years older, was almost totally bald and defiantly corpulent, obviously well satisfied with his bulging stomach and his lot in life. Alex introduced them as Mr. and Mrs. Dillon. "This," he said proudly, "is my daughter, Liz."

Mrs. Dillon's proffered hand felt like a marshmallow. "What a big girl you are to have such a handsome young father!"

Lisette, who knew she was slight by American standards, managed a thin smile and a polite good morning before Mr. Dillon began pumping her arm up and down with a heartiness unquenched by a sleepless night. "I'd say she wasn't any bigger than a minute. But pretty, mighty pretty, for all that."

Removing her hand from the man's moist grip, Lisette backed off but kept on smiling. Nobody except her nanny had ever told her she was pretty, and then only as a reward for being especially good.

"The Dillons are heading for Singapore," Alex said in an effort to get the conversation on a more general footing.

"How interesting," Lisette murmured politely, then turned to Mrs. Dillon. "Is this your first trip to the Far East?"

"No. We've been here a couple of times, because—"

"Can't stay away," interrupted Mr. Dillon. "Great place to pick up Chinese antiques. That is, if you know where to go."

"You're a collector?" Alex asked in a tone of mild surprise.

"Of sorts. You see, we've got this big new house in Dallas, and we thought we'd go Oriental."

"It's quite the vogue," Mrs. Dillon put in.

Her husband frowned. "Vogue or no vogue, I like the stuff. It's got style and it's got history. Besides, there's no place for it to go but up."

Apparently amused by the remark, Alex chuckled. "Right," he agreed.

Standing by quietly, Lisette tried to appraise this florid American. He seemed crude by comparison to the only other collector she knew, a friend of her mother's whose drawing-room cases were filled with Japanese netsukes. Recalling the delicacy with which this gentleman handled the intricately carved ivory objects and the appreciation with which he spoke of them, she wondered what he'd think of Mr. Dillon. Would he find him stupid or merely offensive?

"Make no mistake," Alex told Lisette later, after they had walked back to the plane together and were settled once more in their seats. "Dillon isn't stupid. He's probably a millionaire a dozen times over, and like a good businessman he's chosen a hobby that may prove lucrative as well as interesting."

"Do you like him, Papaul?" Lisette asked.

Alex shrugged. "I neither like him nor dislike him. He's a type of rich Texan, and as a type he interests me superficially." He paused, then continued, "You'll get used to me, Liz. I take up with all sorts of people. I want to know what makes them tick."

"Tick?"

"What makes them behave the way they do."

"Oh." Lisette doubted that she'd ever get used to her father's slang.

"You'll have me talking like a dictionary," her father complained, as though he could read her thoughts.

Before Lisette could reply, the captain's voice asked for the passengers' attention. He sounded apologetic when he explained that the necessary engine part had arrived, but that the installation would take longer than expected. Then he murmured something about a prolonged delay.

Lisette sighed, but her father, like most of the experienced travelers, had grown philosophical. He went in search of a stewardess and came back with a pack of cards in his hand. "Ever play gin rummy, Liz?"

Lisette shook her head.

"I'll teach you," he said. "It'll help pass the time."

Noon came, and the sun blazed down from almost directly overhead, threatening to melt the tarmac, if not the airplane itself. Finally the hatches were closed and seat belts fastened. Relieved at being aloft again, Alex put away the cards, adjusted his chair back, and went to sleep.

Lisette sat beside him feeling lost and wretched. She hated strangeness and strangers, she decided, and above all things she hated long airplane rides. The afternoon hours dragged by as she stared down at a sea of cotton-wool clouds, and when the Bangkok airport finally became visible the sun was setting.

"At last!"

"Long day," agreed Alex, "and it's not over yet. Customs always takes a dim view of the amount of camera equipment I haul along."

So while other passengers were waved through with white chalk marks scratched hastily on their luggage, Lisette stood beside her father impatiently as an inspector made him open every case and ex-

31

plain the contents in detail. Forms had to be filled out, waivers signed, and they left the terminal building with the last stragglers from the flight. Eventually all their luggage was stowed into a decrepit taxi.

Then, through a bilingual airline employee, the driver was instructed to take them to the Grand Palace, the most unlikely address in the city. The driver objected vigorously, shaking his head and gesticulating, and he was still muttering to himself as he swung onto the highway. Obviously he thought these tourists were crazy, but he was prepared to do as he was told.

There was no air conditioning in the cab; the springs in the back seat were broken. Lisette lurched against her father and said, as he righted her, "Sorry, Papaul."

"No matter." Alex patted her shoulder. "The end is near."

After a while he said, "Bet I know what you're thinking about. A cool shower."

Lisette nodded.

"Me too."

The landscape was flat and dusty, in spite of the water-filled ditches bordering the road. Lisette mopped her perspiring face with a soggy cleansing tissue and yawned compulsively, as the taxi rattled into the outskirts of the sprawling city, where lights were already twinkling in the dusk.

As though he were negotiating a maze, the driver made a dozen or more right-angle turns before he pulled up before an impressive gate set in a long, high wall. Inside, dimly visible, was a complex of buildings, but the huge courtyard was empty and the gate was locked. Alex rattled it loudly, shouted hello, and in sign language instructed the driver to unload the luggage. Lisette could see that the man understood but had no intention of doing anything of the kind. He made a sign in the air like a lock turning, shrugged, and shook his head as firmly as he had back at the airport.

"I think he's trying to tell you it's closed," Lisette said.

"I know it's closed, but we're *expected.*" Alex emphasized the word as though the driver could understand. "He thinks we're tourists, trying to get in after hours. He doesn't realize we're going to *live* inside." Again he tried to rattle the heavy iron grille, again he shouted at the top of his lungs, but to no avail. Around the taxi a crowd of street urchins began to gather, watching the antics of the funny foreigner, but from inside the palace wall there wasn't a sound.

The driver climbed back in his cab, lit a cigarette, and settled down to wait. Whenever Alex turned his way he beckoned to him, indicating the rear seat, in which Lisette reinstalled herself.

"Maybe there's another gate, Papaul!"

"Could be. *Another gate?*" he asked the driver loudly, as if raising his voice could force him to understand.

"*Une autre porte?*" tried Lisette in French, although quite naturally Thai was the only language the man could understand. His expression brightened, however, when Alex climbed back inside and slammed the door. He started the motor at once and drove rapidly back toward the river road from which they had come. Then he took matters into his own hands and hurtled toward the center of the city, where lights from some moderately tall buildings winked against the darkening sky. Almost at once the traffic thickened. Buses, automobiles, and bicycles crammed the streets, moving along at a snail's pace when they moved at all.

"Where do you think he's taking us?" Lisette murmured.

"Your guess is as good as mine, but I suppose he'll dump us at some hotel."

Lisette sneezed. She felt alternately hot and cold and was trembling with exhaustion. The thought of a hotel—any hotel offering bath and bed—was inviting.

The taxi inched along for another ten minutes, then turned off the congested street and pulled up at the glass-and-chrome entrance to a huge, tall building. "Indra Regent," said the driver, with a proud wave of his hand, and pointed to a handsome, conspicuous sign.

"Looks OK to me," said Alex, as his eyes roved over the facade. "But don't let him unload our bags, Liz, until I make sure we can get a couple of rooms."

Lisette nodded. Her head had begun to throb and she sneezed again, certain by now that she was catching a cold. Whisked back and forth as she had been from air conditioning to heat, it was no wonder, but it added the final straw to her misery.

In a few minutes Alex returned at a gallop, accompanied by a helpful doorman and a uniformed boy with a luggage cart. With incredible speed the taxi was unloaded, the driver paid, and the bags transported to a suite on the eighteenth floor.

"Pretty swanky," Alex commented, when the door was closed, "but it was the only thing available."

"It looks like heaven to me," Lisette said, as she walked into her bedroom and dropped her shoulder bag on a chair. "Papaul, do you mind if I say goodnight right now? I'm not feeling well."

"You're not? What's wrong?"

The expression on her father's face told Lisette that this was a development for which he was quite unprepared. He had blithely toted his daughter along to Southeast Asia, but he hadn't bargained on her becoming ill.

"Don't worry, Papaul. It's just a cold," Lisette said in an attempt to be comforting.

Alex still looked concerned. "Have you got any aspirin?"

"I don't think so."

"I'll bring you some."

Lisette swallowed two of the white tablets. "I'll probably be quite all right in the morning," she said reassuringly.

The bed sheets felt cool against her burning skin, but a few minutes later she was shivering. Her teeth chattered uncontrollably as she lay huddled under the lightweight blanket, waiting for the chill to subside.

Eventually she fell into a troubled sleep, punctuated with frightening dreams. She stood at the palace gate once more, only now her ankles and wrists were bound, so that she couldn't move. Alex was trying to scale the wall on a rope ladder, unaware that within the palace grounds shadows moved, eerie shapes forming and dissolving. Half-human, half-beast, they prowled menacingly. "Papaul!" Lisette tried to shout. "Papaul, come back!" But no sound came from her throat.

Then, in the nightmare, an enormous fat man with Mr. Dillon's face materialized just beyond the gate's iron grille. Seated cross-legged on a rug that floated a few feet above the ground like a magic carpet, the man's little pig eyes were fixed and staring, his lips curved in a horrible leer. And his face— a mask of evil defying description—was a bright, transparent green.

"I am the Emerald Buddha," the fat man said.

Lisette screamed.

III

Suddenly she was in her father's arms, sitting up in bed and clinging to him while he patted her shoulder soothingly. "Oh, Papaul," she said, sobbing, "I had the most horrible dream!"

"There, there." Alex spoke uncharacteristically, as if he were trying to comfort a small child. "A fever can give you nightmares, but you'll be all right now."

Lisette pulled away from the beard that was tickling her cheek and said, "Of course," feeling ashamed that the first physical gesture of affection she had ever shown her father had come without conscious volition. She was embarrassed and showed it. "I'm sorry," she murmured, as she slipped down beneath the covers again.

Alex went to the window and pulled back the heavy curtains that shut out the light of early morning, light that was both a surprise and a relief to Lisette. "What time is it?" she asked.

"A little after seven." Walking back to the bed, Alex leaned over and felt Lisette's forehead with the flat of his hand. Then he straightened and said sternly, "I'm going to get you a doctor, whether you like it or not."

He telephoned room service from the living room of the suite, ordered breakfast for himself and tea for Lisette, then arranged with a clerk at the hotel desk to have a doctor call. Shortly after nine o'clock there was a knock at the door, and a slight, clean-shaven Thai wearing an immaculate white shirt and dark trousers announced himself as Dr. Kasemset.

Although he spoke only a few words of English, the doctor was professional and very polite. He took

Lisette's temperature, inspected her throat, and felt her pulse, making small commiserating sounds in the back of his throat as he worked. Then he took a bottle of pills from the kit he was carrying, poured a few into a small envelope, and indicated that there was nothing to worry about and that the patient should feel better tomorrow.

"Proong nee," he kept repeating. *Tomorrow.* It was Lisette's first rememberable Thai word.

In parting, after giving instructions concerning the dosage of the pills, Dr. Kasemset advised Lisette to stay in bed, or at least in the suite, for the rest of the day.

"That doesn't mean you have to be cooped up here too," Lisette told her father. "I don't need a nurse."

Alex accepted this statement. "I'd like to get back to the palace and find out what the slipup was," he admitted. "Also, Goodfellow must be wondering what happened to us."

"If he had called the airport," suggested Lisette, "he would have learned that our plane was delayed."

"Right," agreed Alex. "On the other hand, he could be the absentminded-professor type."

After loading a small camera that he was in the habit of carrying with him, and telling Lisette that he'd telephone if he was delayed beyond one o'clock, Alex said good-bye and left. Once the door was shut, the rooms were very still. The sunshine seemed far away, since it was impossible to feel its warmth in the air-conditioned suite. Bells rang somewhere in the distance—temple bells? The muted hum of traffic crept up from the street eighteen stories below. Lisette dozed, then gradually dropped into a deep and restoring sleep.

It was barely noon when she awakened, aroused by a sound of a clicking door latch and the soft scurrying of feet. A diminutive Thai maid hesitated in the doorway before approaching Lisette's bed. She asked an unintelligible question, which probably was, "Are you sick?"

Lisette responded in pantomime, which she suspected she would learn to use with some proficiency before the summer was over. Tucking her hands, palms facing, under one cheek, she leaned on them and shut her eyes descriptively.

The girl's mouth formed an "o" and she backed off, quietly closing the door, but Lisette could hear her scampering around in the adjoining rooms for fifteen minutes or so.

By now, thoroughly awake and feeling much better, Lisette got up, brushed her teeth, soaked briefly in a warm tub, and put on fresh pajamas. Then she plumped up the bed pillows and propped herself against them, reaching for a paperback her father had tucked into her suitcase before leaving New York. It was *Anna and the King of Siam.*

Siam, the old name for Thailand. And Anna, the young, impetuous governess, who had almost lost her liberty, if not her life, in trying to reform and update an absolute monarch for whom the world outside his kingdom was a mystery he did not care to explore. How romantic it all sounded, how incredibly removed from the present and from this huge, flat city of three million people. Lisette had seen the American movie, *The King and I,* at a Paris rerun theater, and she envied the times in which Anna had lived, the marvelous clothes she had worn, and the sense of high adventure with which she was supposed to have challenged life at court.

Before Lisette had read half a chapter the telephone rang. "Hi, Liz! How are you feeling?"

"Much better, Papaul."

"Honestly?"

"Cross my heart."

"Are you hungry?"

"A little," Lisette confessed.

"Good. Order something from room service, will you? I'm heading back to the center of town now, but I have a few contacts I'd like to make before the day's over."

Alex spoke so briskly that Lisette restrained her

curiosity about his reception at the palace. She regretted her forbearance, however, the instant she put the phone down. Had he seen Professor Goodfellow? Had he been shown the quarters where they were to live? And when would they be moving in?

After a few minutes she picked up the receiver again and ordered poached eggs on toast and another pot of tea, then slipped a light nylon robe over her pajamas and knotted its belt around her waist. Although still weak, she felt well on the way to recovery and walked over to the windows to see what she could of this strange, sprawling city that was to be her temporary home.

The view straight down was dizzying. Into a flat rooftop terrace, perhaps fourteen floors below, was set an oblong blue swimming pool surrounded by tables, beach umbrellas, reclining chairs, and a number of people in bathing suits. Were it not for a beautifully carved wooden house placed incongruously at one end of the pool, like an antique doll's house dropped into a contemporary setting, the scene could have been photographed at almost any big resort hotel.

Beyond the lower roof, however, the buildings of Bangkok's crowded market district straggled off under a heat haze that painted them ocher and gray. A few spiked rooftops, probably belonging to temples, thrust upward, but did little to alleviate the monotonous skyline.

So this was Bangkok! Lisette wondered what actually she had expected. Elephants and palanquins? Silken robes and pagodalike houses? She had been thinking in terms of Anna's Siam, if she had thought at all.

There was a discreet knock at the door. Food! Lisette crossed the room and admitted a waiter with a rolling cart, which he set up ceremoniously in front of the most comfortable chair. Sunk in its depths with her chin almost touching the tablecloth, Lisette ate the poached eggs with relish and sipped two cups of tea.

Then she leaned back in the chair and let her mind drift at random. She could write a letter to Philippe, but what was there to say? *Nous sommes arrivés à Bangkok. Je suis desenchantée avec la ville, peut être parce que—*

It wasn't worthwhile to make the effort, but once her thoughts had turned to Philippe they turned inevitably to Brittany, to rock pools and shrimping nets and the smell of the sea. There was a little cove where they sometimes picnicked on sand as flat and fine as a carpet. Lisette remembered the yellow flowers that grew in a fault in the rocks, the feel of the ocean breeze against her tanned skin, the bleached hairs on Philippe's forearms as he lay on his stomach telling her about something that had happened at school.

There was another knock at the door. Expecting the waiter to return for the cart, she had left the door unlocked. *"Entrez,"* Lisette called. The man who turned the knob and stood on the threshold, however, was no Thai servant. He was tall, blond, impeccably dressed in a gray tropical suit, and as unmistakably British as though he had been carrying a Union Jack.

"I beg your pardon, *mam'selle*," he said with unhurried poise. "Perhaps I have the wrong room. I am looking for Mr. Alexander Paul."

Lisette pushed back the table and stood up. "This is the right room," she answered. "Mr. Paul is my father, but he isn't in."

"Ah!" The Englishman took a step or two forward. "Then I've missed him. How unfortunate." He hesitated for a moment, then asked, "Are you expecting him back soon?"

Uncomfortably aware that pajamas and robe were an odd costume in which to be entertaining a visitor, especially one who looked rather distinguished, Lisette replied, "I really don't know."

"Ah," said the Englishman again. Although he didn't close the door behind him, he seemed in no hurry to leave. "Let me introduce myself, Miss Paul." He took a wallet from his pocket and extracted a calling card, coming forward to hand it to Lisette. "Courtney Hood," he said. "Perhaps I could leave your father a note."

"Of course," Lisette replied, as she glanced down at the oblong white card. There was an address printed at the lower left corner, and on the right she read, "Oriental Antiquities."

While Mr. Hood was searching through his pockets for paper on which to write, the waiter returned to collect the cart. He wheeled it out and closed the door discreetly behind him, as the Englishman asked, "Is there a hotel pad or perhaps some stationery I might use?"

Lisette opened the drawers of a flat-topped desk and found a folded blotter with letter paper and postcards inside. Mr. Hood, with a conventional "May I?" seated himself in the desk chair, crossed his gray-trousered legs, and took a pen from his inside jacket pocket. He glanced at his watch, noted the time, smiled across at Lisette, who had settled into the big chair again, and started to write.

When he had finished the note he folded the paper, slipped it into an envelope, and placed it near the desk lamp, before returning the blotter to the drawer. He did everything deliberately, as though he were in no hurry whatsoever. Indeed, Lisette thought, he seems to be dawdling in the hope that my father will return.

"I'll just leave this here," said Mr. Hood, touching the envelope with a fingertip. "I shall be very happy to make your father's acquaintance, Miss Paul. He is a superb photographer."

"I think so too!" Lisette responded spontaneously. She had not yet learned to take her father for granted.

"I am hoping to persuade him to photograph my private collection," continued Mr. Hood. "In his spare time, of course."

Lisette felt that some comment was called for, but she didn't feel she should voice her doubts that her father would have any free hours. Instead, she asked, "Do you collect—paintings?"

"A few," replied Mr. Hood with an amiable smile, "but I'm mainly interested in sculpture. I'm a merchant, you see. I buy and sell. But some very special pieces—those I find irresistible—I keep for myself."

Lisette felt out of her depth, although she was flattered that Mr. Hood was talking to her as to an adult. She was glad, however, when he changed the subject and said, "I understand you're to be staying in one of the guest villas at the palace?"

"I believe so."

"You should be quite comfortable, I'd say. Tell

me, has your father met Professor Goodfellow?"

"Not yet," Lisette admitted. She was tempted to tell Mr. Hood about last evening's fiasco at the palace gate but her natural shyness kept her silent.

"Ah," said Mr. Hood with a sudden twinkle in his eye, "he has a treat in store."

This remark puzzled Lisette, but she was too polite to say so. She kept wishing Mr. Hood would leave, but instead he considered Lisette reflectively.

"I say, you don't look in the least American."

"My mother is French."

"Ah, that explains the '*entrez*.'"

In a faintly teasing manner, Lisette said, "You are perceptive, Mr. Hood."

Quite seriously he replied, "One must try to be in Southeast Asia. There are many pitfalls for the uninitiated, as poor Jim Thompson discovered. To his destruction, I might add."

Mr. Hood glanced at his watch once more, apparently decided he should wait no longer in the hope that Alexander Paul might show up, thanked Lisette for her courtesy, bowed, and departed. Less than ten minutes later Alex bounded through the door, as full of energy as a boxer puppy.

"Liz, you're up! Feeling better, I hope?"

"Much better, Papaul," said Lisette. She handed her father Mr. Hood's card. "You had a visitor."

49

Alex glanced at the name. "Oh yes. A well-known dealer. Wonder what he wants of me?"

"He wants you to photograph his art collection in your spare time. There's a note from him on the desk."

"What spare time?" Alex muttered. He read the note, shrugged, then glanced at Lisette appraisingly. "You feel up to moving, or should we take these rooms for another night?"

Sensing that her father might want to avoid the extra expense, Lisette gathered her courage. "I think I can make it."

"Good girl. Get into some clothes, but don't hurry. Want me to help you pack?"

Lisette shook her head. "No, thanks." From the door to her bedroom she asked, "Papaul, have you ever heard of a man called Jim Thompson?"

En route to his own room her father called, "Sure. I'll tell you all about his strange disappearance—but some other time."

Half an hour later a porter was trundling the Pauls' baggage along the sidewalk in front of the hotel doors, then helping Lisette into a cab that proved more comfortable than the one in which she and her father had arrived. In the daylight the city looked even more nondescript than it had at dark. To a stranger's eyes it was a scene of chaos, people crowding the streets and the intersections, car brakes squealing, horns tooting, traffic again snarled. Yet Lisette noted that the Thai faces she could pick out of the throng were smiling and relatively serene. To be so cheerful in the midst of this maddening din seemed incredible.

After the cab left the market district the taxi driver made good time. Within twenty minutes he pulled up at the gate on Sanam Chai Road that led into the palace grounds. At midafternoon it was open, and the guard on duty recognized Mr. Paul. He helped unload the luggage and gave it to the safe-keeping of two uniformed boys no taller than Lisette. These porters led them through courtyards lined with curious and impressive buildings, past stupas, temples, and pavilions guarded by monumental statues of demons and elephants. Such color and variety was bewitching. Contemporary Bangkok no longer existed. This was another world!

"Quite a layout." Alex chortled. "What do you make of it, Liz?"

"It's like a fairy tale," Lisette breathed. Within the battlemented walls high-spired structures crowded one another, shimmering in the sunlight, and from any one of them Lisette felt that a prince or princess might emerge.

Instead, a shaven-headed yellow-robed monk hurried along under a colonnade that led to still another pagoda. He shot an incurious glance at the porters but ignored the Americans and disappeared quickly, his robe fluttering behind him like the plumage of an exotic bird.

"I've learned a few things about this compound. The king no longer lives here, but the Grand Palace is still used for special ceremonies," said Alex, as he suited his stride to Lisette's slower pace. "In the old days it was divided into two separate sections, the Outside, where we are now, and the Inside, which was strictly private. The king's wives, along with their children and ladies-in-waiting, lived in the Inside, where no man but the monarch himself was permitted to enter. Apparently the flower gardens and fountains and little villas they used still exist. We'll be staying in one of them."

"How fortunate," murmured Lisette.

"I'll say. I don't know how Goodfellow managed it."

The sun disappeared so suddenly that Lisette glanced up at the sky. Thunderclouds were gathering overhead, causing the young porters to shift their burdens and hasten their steps, as they cut across a courtyard to an area protected by a high wrought-iron fence. A very old man, with a face like a withered almond shell, was waiting at a gate to receive

52

Lisette and her father with all of the courtesy reserved for distinguished visitors. Dressed entirely in white, he looked frail and insubstantial, yet Lisette noticed that his eyes were lively and appraising. Ceremoniously he turned a heavy key and swung the portal back. As he led the visitors along an empty street lined with square sandstone houses that looked faintly suburban, Alex murmured, "Bet that old boy doesn't miss much."

"Are we in the private compound now?"

"We are indeed."

Lisette felt mildly disappointed. The villas lacked the fantasy of the buildings on the Outside. The elderly caretaker stopped at the third in the row and opened a teak door with a smaller key, which he handed to Alex just as thunder roared overhead and rain started to fall in a silver deluge.

"Just an afternoon shower," Alex decided. "By the way, Liz, you take off your shoes before you go inside. It's an old Thai custom. As I said, I'm learning."

The interior of the house was dim and cool compared to the steaming air outside. A young female servant appeared and said something to the porters, who set off in different directions, one carrying Lisette's two suitcases and the other hauling Alex's camera equipment as well as his bulky gear.

53

Apparently the villa had been modernized to accommodate foreign visitors. The furniture, except for some beautiful antique carved chests, was primarily Western, and the bed in Lisette's room looked comfortable. The maid hurried across the floor and threw open the shutters, giggling up at the stormy sky. She giggled again when Lisette threw her purse on the bed and turned to inspect the bathroom, which had simple but adequate plumbing. Besides, it was private, a delightful boon!

Suddenly Lisette felt weak and tottery. Realizing she had been overexerting in an effort to be a good sport, she sank down on the edge of the bed just as Alex appeared in the doorway. "Going to be comfortable enough?"

"Oh yes," replied Lisette.

"Still feel a little weak?"

"A little."

"Why don't you lie down? If the rain stops, I'll go exploring, but I won't be far away."

Such consideration surprised Lisette. She closed the door, slipped out of her dress, and threw herself across the bed in her panties and bra, falling asleep almost at once. When she awakened, the storm was over and the sun was setting. As the New York editor had predicted, the air was washed and clear.

Unpacking could wait until morning. Bathing and

dressing took very little time. As Lisette appeared in the salon her father was just coming through the door. He looked elated.

"Wait till you really see this joint!" he cried. "Sixty pictures? I could take six hundred! It's got everything. Color, atmosphere, style, and a sort of undefinable mystery. It's great!"

From the open doorway behind him came a low, throaty chuckle. "I was sure you'd like it," a woman's voice said.

As her father swung around Lisette saw, over his shoulder, a tall, sunburned young woman whose wheat-colored hair touched her shoulders. Wearing a straw hat pushed to the back of her head, she was dressed in a faded blue cotton shift, sleeveless and unbelted. Her legs were bare and brown, and as she kicked off her sandals Lisette noticed that her toenails were painted. Conspicuously American, she looked healthy, relaxed, and frankly amused.

"Oh Lord, a beard!" she said, as she approached Alex with outstretched hand. "How to be conspicuous in Thailand!"

Taken aback, Alex asked bluntly, "Who are *you?*"

The young woman laughed. "Kyle Goodfellow, of course. And this must be your daughter?"

IV

As the young woman turned to Lisette, Alex made a vain attempt to stifle his surprise. Abruptly he gave up and burst out laughing. "This isn't fair! You're supposed to be a man, Professor Goodfellow."

"Kyle. Let's not stand on ceremony. And this is—?"

"Liz," said Lisette's father.

"Hi, Liz. I hope they've made you comfortable."

"Very, thank you."

"And I apologize for not being here when you arrived, but I had a chance to go out to the summer palace and interview a scholar who could answer some very important questions about the Wat Phra Keo."

"The what?" asked Alex with an obvious play on words.

"The Temple of the Emerald Buddha. It's very special, as you'll soon see."

The Emerald Buddha again! Lisette felt haunted by an unseen presence. Was he a person or an image? She wanted to ask but restrained herself for fear of sounding foolish.

"A temple is called a *wat* in Thai," Kyle was explaining, as though teaching was her second nature. Then she cried, including Lisette in her welcome, "I *am* glad to see you!"

"And now that the shock is over, I'm glad you're not a man," Alex replied easily.

With the preliminaries out of the way, Kyle immediately got down to business. "Apparently you've had a chance to look around, Alex?"

"Just came back from a quick tour."

"And you're really enthusiastic?"

"It's marvelous—bigger than I expected—"

"Covers nearly a square mile," Kyle observed.

"—but it's made to order for a picture book!"

Lisette stood by and listened for a while, then slipped into the shadows and perched on a straight chair of vaguely Oriental design. She was captivated by Kyle Goodfellow's appearance, by her casual clothes, her youthful American directness, and the shine in her wide-set brown eyes. She wasn't pretty exactly, but she was attractive and very outgoing. That she was old enough to have earned a doctorate and the title of professor seemed remarkable.

As the conversation progressed Lisette gathered that Kyle was an authority on Thai art and sculpture, and on the Grand Palace in particular. Since her enthusiasm over the project seemed to equal Alex's, they were bound to make a great team.

Although Lisette, in her role of spectator, was ignored by the collaborators, she, too, felt a stirring of anticipation. It would be interesting to watch her father at work, to stand by and see an idea grow into a book. For the first time the thought occurred to her that although she might not have an entertaining summer, at least she would have an educational one.

"I'd like to take you both on an orientation trip tomorrow morning before the tourists arrive," Kyle proposed over dinner, which was served by the same giggly maid who had shown Lisette to her room. "Then, after you learn your way around the palace complex, Alex, we can discuss the sequence of shots."

Lisette set the alarm on her travel clock when she went to bed, but awakened before it went off. Breakfast appeared on a tray while she was dressing. Canned juice, tea, a sweetish roll. Everything tasted good. It was lovely to be feeling well again.

The early morning air was far from crisp, but it was bearable in contrast to the sultriness of yesterday afternoon. Kyle and her father were already at the door, impatient to be off, when Lisette ran downstairs. They were talking together like old friends, alive with plans and enthusiasm. Lisette detected a new sparkle in her father's blue eyes.

"The book should have a flow; don't you agree?" he asked Kyle. "In the photographs as well as in the text." He was carrying no camera equipment, which seemed surprising, until he explained that he never started work until he had the whole setup firmly in mind.

Lisette felt faintly jealous of this dynamic young woman who had captured her father's attention so completely that she herself might have been invisible. Alex obviously attracted Kyle. Not only his professional ability but his personality made her appreciate him.

Raised in a world of women, both at the manoir and the convent, Lisette was unaccustomed to having men around. Philippe was a dear, but he was still too immature to be compared to her father, whose youthful cheekiness and audacity did not conceal his maturity.

That women might find Alex intriguing, Lisette hadn't anticipated, so the idea came as something of a shock. She began to look at him in a new light and to understand how, long ago, he could have swept her mother off her feet.

A towering demon guardian twenty feet high stood directly ahead. Kyle and Alex skirted it with a mere glance, but Lisette stopped to consider the carved facial expression, which looked both fierce and benevolent.

"Better not lag behind," called Kyle, as she led the way from one enclosure to the next. "Until you know your way around, you could get hopelessly lost."

Lisette ran a few steps to catch up, in time to hear Kyle say, "Almost all of these places have been altered. According to Thai Buddhist beliefs, rebuilding earns more merit than restoring or mere preservation."

"Yes, Professor," said Alex, an assumed meekness masking the teasing note in his voice.

Kyle hesitated, but didn't change her tone. "I'll make one exception. The Temple of the Emerald Buddha probably looks much as it always did."

"Why is that?" Alex grew more serious.

"Because it's Thailand's number one shrine. The Buddha has been here forever—almost two hundred years."

One question settled, thought Lisette. "Then he's not alive," she said aloud.

"Heavens, no!" Kyle laughed. "The Buddha is made of pure jade in the most glorious emerald-green color. Nobody knows where it actually came from, but it's famous for surviving all sorts of catastrophes —war, fires, flood, even theft."

Alex made no effort to stifle a yawn. His alert eyes took in every possible picture, but background detail seemed to bore him.

Not in the least discountenanced, Kyle said to Lisette, "There are some wonderful stories about the Buddha. I'll tell them to you someday. You'll see why this image is truly revered by the Thai people. They believe it has a divine force of its own."

Lisette shuddered ever so slightly as a thrill of apprehension ran down her spine. There was something exaggerated and mysterious about this vast palace complex, something forbidding about the giant statues, which frowned and grinned at her. She felt as vulnerable as Alice in Wonderland, shrunken to a size little larger than a mouse.

"I'm anxious to see your star boarder," Alex was saying to Kyle. "Think it's possible to get a color shot of the Buddha for the book jacket?"

Kyle looked doubtful. "It's a great idea, but there's a rule that no pictures can be taken inside the chapel."

"Aren't rules like that made for tourists?"

"Perhaps. I can consult the powers that be."

"By that do you mean the king?"

"Heavens, no. I have no direct access to the king," Kyle said, "but I can sound out some of the museum people and the man who heads up the resident staff."

She stopped, her hand on a balustrade, looking thoughtful. "I don't know what their reaction will be," she admitted. "It would be an honor to have a picture of the Buddha on a book of this importance, if they happen to see it that way. On the other hand, they protect it fiercely and might not give an inch."

"OK." Alex didn't quibble. "So we'll step lightly for a while."

"On tiptoe, I'd suggest."

Lisette was growing impatient. "Can we see the Buddha this morning?" she dared to ask.

"If the doors are open," Kyle replied. Then she added, "We have plenty of time."

Resuming her professorial tone, Kyle became involved in descriptions of the courtyards through which they were walking. Lisette, meanwhile, gazed up at the spires shining like jewels against the blue sky and occasionally paused to inspect curious bronze lions, elephants, oxen, and monkeys that ornamented every turn.

"Modern workmanship, but rather good," Kyle said in passing. "Thai sculptors have a knack with animal expressions, don't you think?"

By now the sun was quite high in the east, and the trio no longer had the palace to themselves. On the pavement of a big square bounded by time-worn buildings, sweepers were swinging primitive brooms made of stiff bundles of straw. In this particular yard, stands were being set up with wares consisting of postcards, knickknacks, souvenirs of Thailand, and some charming, cheap-metal replicas of the bronze temple bells that chimed sweetly with every gust of air.

Lisette sniffed a strange, foreign aroma and noticed a food stall with a charcoal brazier, heard the clink of bottles arriving for a soft drink stand. In the shadow of a building a legless cripple unrolled a sheaf of rubbings, and a young man propped half a dozen watercolors against a window ledge.

"The palace gates must be open," Kyle murmured,

checking her watch. "Let's cut through here and get to the Wat Phra Keo before the tourists beat us to it!"

She walked quickly, with long, free strides, in step with Alex, while Lisette trotted along behind. At last! she thought, quite forgetting the fat man in her dream and thinking only of the emerald-jade image Kyle was about to introduce.

Expecting a single temple, Lisette was surprised when she climbed broad steps to a huge terrace studded with glistening golden towers, timbered halls, and pagodas decorated as lavishly as wedding cakes. Around the enormous compound ran a covered gallery, where several artists were at work restoring flaking wall paintings.

Kyle ignored them. She went directly toward a tall structure with a three-tiered roof, a building so magnificent that it appeared to shimmer in the sunlight. Figures of Chinese guardians riding on lions flanked a great door with panels inlaid with mother-of-pearl. "The Temple of the Emerald Buddha," announced Kyle, as though she were presenting them to a royal personage.

Alex whistled softly. His eyes moved in admiration over the intricate facade, but Lisette noticed only that the huge door was closed and bolted.

Aware of her disappointment, Kyle explained

quickly. "This central door may be used only **by** the king and queen. Ordinary mortals like us **enter** through the one on the left."

Lisette then noticed that the door she indicated was ajar. A slight Thai man in an official-looking uniform was straining to push it open further. Kyle hailed him as if they were on friendly terms, and he smiled back at her and bowed politely. After a brief exchange in what Lisette assumed was Thai, he bowed again to Alex and Lisette, then stood aside.

Kyle kicked off her sandals and dropped them on the steps. Lisette followed suit, and Alex pulled off his loafers and parked them with unexpected neatness under a bench. Inside, the chapel was so dimly lighted that Lisette had to blink her eyes several times to adjust to the dark after the brilliant sunlight.

Only gradually did she become aware of a shimmering altar flanked by two large crowned Buddha statues covered with gold. Then her eyes inevitably were drawn up—up and up—past demon guardians and glittering trees of gold and silver to the figure seated in a tiny pavilion under five golden crowns that diminished in scale as they rose toward an umbrella-shaped canopy. Two glass balls, one representing the sun and the other the moon, hung on either side of the image but they meant nothing to

Lisette. It was the Buddha, carved of the purest opalescent green jade, which was remarkable. Its twenty-four-inch height was so relatively small that it was like a fabulous toy reigning over all this gigantic magnificence.

The doll-like quality was enhanced by the fact that it was dressed. "Oh look, he's wearing clothes!" Lisette couldn't help exclaiming.

Kyle smiled. "Yes. There are three changes of clothing. This is the rainy-season costume, rather like a monk's robe."

"A pretty fancy monk's robe," muttered Alex. "What's it made of—crocheted gold?"

"Gold and blue enamel. It's the simplest of the Buddha's three costumes, I understand. The others are said to be studded with precious stones."

"Does he wear different hats, too?" Lisette asked.

Kyle nodded. "Speaking of precious stones," she said, "this particular headdress is covered with jewels. We're too far away to see, but they're spiraling clockwise. I brought my binoculars over the other day and got a really close look."

In the enormous room, where they seemed to be the only occupants, although a guard was doubtless hovering in the background, all three had instinctively lowered their voices to a whisper. In spite of its small size, the jade Buddha was very commanding. As her father and Kyle moved closer to the altar, Lisette stood gazing up at the enigmatic figure and tried to fix it in her mind's eye.

One shoulder and arm were bare, but both crossed legs were swathed to the ankles by the golden robe. The hands, palms upward, were folded serenely in the lap. Drooping eyelids all but covered the eyes, and the nose was broad and flat, as wide as the full-lipped mouth, which might have seemed cherubic had the Buddha worn a smile. Instead, it looked solemn and remote, lost in contemplation as it sat impassively on its elaborate throne.

The silence was suddenly shattered by a loud and vigorous sneeze, so unexpected and close to Lisette's ear that she started and stepped back before she realized that it came from directly behind her. She felt the impact of a body and heard a tinkling clatter, as a shower of small objects hit the copper-tiled floor.

"Oh, *excusez-moi!*" Lisette cried softly, trying to conceal her momentary fright. Then she glanced down at a handful of coins, which had landed at her feet, before she looked up again at a shaggy-haired boy wearing patched blue jeans and a rumpled shirt.

"I say, I *am* sorry! I must have rather startled you."

"You did," Lisette admitted, as she moved to help

the boy pick up some of the coins that had rolled away. She noticed that he looked about Philippe's age and sounded vaguely English. He appeared amused rather than sorry. Laugh lines crinkled the corners of his eyes, and his mouth twitched in a barely suppressed smile.

"I rarely chuck my money around like this," he explained, as he accepted the last of the coins from Lisette. "I was fishing for a handkerchief, you see."

Lisette didn't reply. The incident over, her habitual shyness returned, and she started to walk away. The boy, however, was not so easily put off. He followed along doggedly and said, "You're French, aren't you? But you do speak English awfully well!"

"I am half American," Lisette replied primly. The nuns had warned her about talking to strangers— any stranger.

"Ah, that explains it!" said the boy happily. "What do you think of the Lord Buddha up there?"

Lisette couldn't find the right words of praise. "I am seeing it for the first time," she replied in a tone indicating dismissal.

"The first and the last most likely. Tourists come for an hour or two, then go." He shrugged. "Too bad."

In spite of herself, Lisette's interest was caught. "You live here then?"

"I camp here."

"Oh." Now what, Lisette wondered, did he mean by that? Seeing her father in the distance, she said, "I must go," and hastened toward him, but half an hour later, as the chapel was beginning to fill with visitors and Kyle decided that it was time to leave, she came upon the boy again. He was standing well back from the throng, looking up at the Buddha.

His study was not so intent, however, that he didn't see Lisette approach. "Hi," he said, smiling in recognition. "I say, did you ever happen to see a movie called *Topkapi?*"

"As a matter of fact, I did," Lisette replied, as her father glanced at the lad in frank puzzlement.

"Great, wasn't it, the way they managed to swipe that big jewel? I was just wondering how a couple of chaps might pull off a trick like that here."

"Cinchy," said Alex, who often spoke to strangers as if they were old friends. "There's a very handy ladder at the back of the throne."

The boy shook his head. "Only the king goes up that," he said, "when he changes the Buddha's clothes."

V

Back at the villa, a pot of yellow orchids stood on a table near the entrance. With it was a card addressed to Miss Kyle Goodfellow, Miss Lisette and Mr. Alexander Paul, containing an invitation to dinner the following evening, from Courtney Hood.

Kyle was pleased. "I understand he has a fascinating house, with some very good pieces of Khmer sculpture," she said, and upon receiving the Pauls' approval, telephoned to say they would be delighted to accept.

Mr. Hood arranged to have a car call for them, saying that taxi drivers always had trouble finding his house, which was situated outside the city limits. As the hour approached eight the following evening, Lisette once again found herself driving through the dusty streets of the teeming city.

Close-packed buildings eventually gave way to blocks of apartments hedged about with colonies of shacks. In passing, Lisette noticed open lots, a high-rise building under construction, and a new factory set on barren ground. It was scarcely a prepossessing neighborhood, and it didn't seem to improve as the lights of the city disappeared behind.

Conversation was desultory. Kyle and Alex had been working together all day while Lisette finished unpacking and wrote long letters to her mother and Philippe. Because the car was air-conditioned, a great luxury, everyone seemed content to ride along quietly and gather energy for the evening ahead.

Although glad to be included in the dinner invitation, Lisette was vaguely dissatisfied with the dress she had chosen to wear, a sleeveless blue linen new last summer but faded from the Brittany sun.

Kyle had put on a long skirt of yellow Thai cotton that matched her shining hair. She looked very chic and sophisticated to Lisette, in contrast to her father, who wore a white sport shirt and checked trousers, spurning both jacket and tie.

The car crossed a bridge over a riverbed to which the rainy season had brought a few feet of water. Then the driver turned off the highway into a lumpy road lined with leafy trees. By now it was almost dark, but the surroundings were still ill-favored. Alex stirred and said, "This looks like the boondocks for sure."

Before anyone spoke again, the car made a sharp turn into a lane bordered by a high stone wall rampant with tangled vines. Then the driver swung through an open gate and pulled up before the entrance to a house that looked, in this tropical setting, completely unreal.

It was modern, made of native stone and glass, so contemporary and dramatic that Lisette caught her breath. Kyle was equally impressed. "Well, well, *well!*" she murmured appreciately.

"What you can do with a magic carpet!" remarked Alex, conveying the impression that the house might well have materialized from thin air.

The man who pushed open a glass sliding door and came to the top of shallow stone steps to greet his guests was real enough, however. Courtney Hood, wearing a black shirt of Thai silk and immaculate white trousers, looked very much at home. "Welcome," he called, and bowed over Kyle's hand in a conventional continental manner. To Lisette, he said, "You look charming tonight, my dear. I hope the cold is quite gone?"

"Quite, thank you." Lisette found herself in a room that combined the qualities of a museum and a garden, although furnished with handsome contemporary couches and chairs. Here and there, discreetly lighted, were ancient sculptures—most of them fragments of statues—that seemed to fit easily into the modern setting.

Mr. Hood introduced the newcomers to a rather commanding Englishwoman, who wore her heavy brown hair in a coronet of braids, then to his secretary, a beautiful Thai girl, who immediately attached herself to Alex and began a conversation in English. Finally they met a tall, thin Cambodian man with a face like a clever fox and a mole on his left cheek. He drew Kyle away from the others and began talking to her in Thai.

Lisette felt rather *de trop*. She could join her father or Kyle or talk to the Englishwoman, whose name she had failed to catch, but everyone seemed suddenly adult and unapproachable.

Quickly Mr. Hood came to her rescue, saying, "There's a young man I want you to meet, Lisette, the son of an old friend. He's having a swim at the moment, but—" Tapping his forehead with the heel of his hand, he interjected, "Why didn't I suggest that you bring a bathing suit?"

Nothing would have pleased Lisette more. The thought of a dip in a swimming pool was like a lovely gift offered and immediately withdrawn, but she simply smiled and murmured something polite and forgiving. At least it was a comfort to know there would be another young person at the dinner party, someone who would presumably talk about something other than Cambodian or Siamese art.

Aperitifs were served by a manservant dressed in a white-duck uniform with a Nehru collar and wearing white gloves, a nicety Lisette had never before encountered, even in the drawing rooms of her mother's wealthiest friends. She asked for a *citron presse* and was rewarded with a drink made not from squeezed lemons, but from fresh lime juice, combined with sugar and soda water in perfect proportions.

"That looks cool!" said a voice at her elbow. "Could I have one of the same?" A boy with roughly toweled hair and a sunburned nose introduced himself by saying, "I'm Don Hall," then whistled in

75

astonishment. "I say, you're the girl who bumped into me in the Temple of the Emerald Buddha! Fancy meeting you *here!*"

"Aha, you've found each other. This is Lisette Paul, Don, the French-American girl I was telling you about."

"We're already acquainted," said Don. "In a manner of speaking, that is."

Mr. Hood didn't ask for particulars. Murmuring, "Splendid, splendid," he went off to join Alex, who was examining a torso that reminded Lisette of some of the Greek statues in the Louvre.

"Ah, I see you are considering my Khmer sculpture with a photographer's eye!" she heard Mr. Hood say to her father. "I'm hoping to induce you to go further."

At that moment the servant returned with a tray bearing a single tall glass. He bowed ever so slightly in front of Lisette's companion, and the rest of Mr. Hood's sales talk was lost.

"Have you seen the pool?" asked Don, as soon as he was handed his drink. "It's bonzer! Come take a look." Lisette obediently followed him through a library and across a long dining room, with a table already laid for dinner, to another set of sliding glass doors. The outside air was moist and heavy after the dry coolness of the house. It felt like velvet against her skin; velvet, too, was the dark-blue sky overhead, embroidered by a few bright stars. In the midst of a tropical walled garden was a free-form pool crossed by an arched Oriental bridge. On the far side were lounge chairs and low tables, and in the clear water close to her feet a few hibiscus flowers floated.

"It's like something out of a Hollywood cinema," Lisette said.

"Quite a contrast to beautiful downtown Bangkok," Don agreed.

"Is this where you're camping?" Lisette ventured curiously.

"Crikey, no! I've got a pup tent on the riverbank over near the palace."

"Then why didn't you come in the car with us?"

"Because I've been here since noon doing my laundry. Every couple of weeks Mr. Hood lets me." He glanced down at his khakis and immaculate shirt. "Don't I look clean?"

Lisette smiled, nodded, then asked, "What's that?" indicating a bracelet on his wrist.

Don twisted it lingeringly. "My good-luck piece. It's made of elephant hair."

"Oh." Lisette asked politely, "Are you a hippie?" She had learned the term, long outmoded in the United States, from her friends at school and had seen hippies in the streets of Paris. They were usually strung with beads and amulets.

Don flicked the bracelet halfway up his arm. "Only a semihippie," he said teasingly.

"Which means you don't smoke pot or take drugs?"

Don burst out laughing. "Coo-ee!" he cried, startling a sleeping bird into song. "If my pop could hear you! I'm just here on my winter vacation. Then it's back to Melbourne and school."

"So you're Australian."

"Couldn't you guess?"

"By your accent? It could be English."

Don shook his head. "My pop has a sheep station outside of Brisbane. I was born there." Indicating the chairs on the far side of the pool, he said, "Let's sit down. They won't be serving dinner for at least half an hour." An idea occurred to him. "Give me your glass. I'll get us another drink."

When he returned, Lisette was sitting on the side of the pool, dangling her feet in the cool water. She reached up and took the fresh drink with a smile of thanks, then said, "I'm glad we've met again. I was curious about you."

"You're a rather curious sort, aren't you?" asked Don, as he crossed his legs Indian fashion and sank down beside her.

Lisette looked surprised. "I suppose I am," she admitted. "I was just going to ask—"

"Hey, it's my turn," interrupted Don. "*I* was just going to ask, what are you doing here?"

Lisette told him about her father's job and their unusual living arrangements. "And I took you for a run-of-the-mill tourist." Don chuckled. "Well, one lives and learns."

He put the glass he was holding down on the pool deck, swung his long legs out straight, and leaned back on his elbows. "Have you been sightseeing yet?"

Lisette shook her head. "We just arrived a few days ago. Besides, my father and Professor Good-fellow aren't here to play. They're working very hard."

"I'll take you around for a day," Don proposed, as if he felt sorry for her. "I've got a good guidebook, and I don't charge a fee."

Through the glass dining-room doors they saw a servant lighting candles. "I think it's time to go inside," said Lisette, and got up, dancing up and down on the cool tiles until her feet dried. She rather liked the custom of leaving shoes at the doorway. To go barefoot was very comfortable in this climate. Besides, it was like being on a picnic instead of at a dinner party.

At the table, Kyle was seated on Courtney Hood's left, the Englishwoman on his right, but Kyle was the one to whom he directed most of his attention. From the other end of the table, Lisette watched her admiringly. She wondered whether she would ever acquire such social ease and marveled that Kyle's erudition did not overshadow her attractiveness. She seemed to slip effortlessly from speaking English to conversing in Thai with the Cambodian, who sat on her other side. Alex was obliged to make conversation with the Englishwoman, whose name Lisette never caught, but he glanced at Kyle frequently. Conversation still hovered about the subject of art and the guests' admiration of Mr. Hood's fine collection. "Where do you find such remarkable pieces?" the Englishwoman asked in a ringing tone that effectively silenced the other guests. "They're surely of museum quality, aren't they, Miss Goodfellow?"

"Yes, indeed," agreed Kyle.

"Then why aren't they in museums?" she persisted.

"Some of them may find their way there eventually," said Mr. Hood with a polite smile.

"Thai museums?"

"Rarely. You see most of my pieces are Cambodian not Thai."

Returning to her original question, the woman asked, "And how do you come by them?"

"By various means." Mr. Hood was still polite, but as he sat back in his chair he heaved a sigh. "Men who know of my interest in Khmer sculpture bring it to me in all sorts of ways—by lorry, automobile, donkey back. One big piece I sold last year came in on an elephant."

"Is that legal?" she asked.

Mr. Hood smiled blandly. "The question of legality must be weighed along with the question of the preservation of valuable antiques. When a man comes across a fragment of a stone statue in the jungle, he's not apt to hand it over free to the Government. If he can get money for it—and I pay well!—he will spirit it across the border without a prick of conscience."

"What about your own conscience, Mr. Hood?" The Englishwoman's question was pertinent but unmannerly.

Still smiling, Mr. Hood picked up his empty wine glass and signaled to a servant to refill it. "My dear lady, I must admit it troubles me very little. Would you rather an important artifact be lost to the world or arrive at a safe resting place nefariously?"

A good point, Lisette thought, following the dialogue with interest. Still, Mr. Hood was avoiding the primary question: was it legal? Or was he, in fact, buying stolen goods?

At this point the Cambodian entered the conversation. "I think it may be said," he suggested in careful English, "that people become very, very *national* about art. Granted that most of my countrymen are unsophisticated concerning the importance of antique torsos sunk in the detritus of the jungle, and granted that it is better to have them rescued than lost, one still does not like to see them leave the country of origin. Witness the Elgin marbles, Mr. Hood. Greece has never quite forgiven England for acquiring them. Is that not true?"

Mr. Hood shrugged. "I guess possession is still nine points of the law."

"In that case, my dear sir, perhaps you have rendered a service—to us all."

"Hear, hear!" The young secretary raised her glass in an unexpected toast.

Mr. Hood bowed in the girl's direction, took a sip of wine, and accepted the opportunity to change the subject. "Have I told you that my charming secretary is something of a treasure herself? She won a beauty contest last year and is now known in her home city of Chieng Mai as Miss Chieng Mai."

The girl blushed prettily, and Kyle murmured something complimentary. Then she said to the Cambodian, "I long to see the Angkor Wat. The model at the palace only whets my appetite. What a pity the site of the ruins is closed."

Mr. Hood shot an appreciative glance in her direction. Kyle had followed his lead and stifled the Englishwoman's persistence in a very graceful way.

Don Hall, however, was bored. He glanced at Lisette and wrinkled his sunburned nose descriptively. "After dinner," he whispered, "I'm going to ask your father if I can take you on the *khlongs*."

"The *khlongs*?"

"The canals. To see the floating markets. Are you game to get up early? Launches leave the Oriental Hotel landing at seven o'clock."

Before Lisette had a chance to answer, Mr. Hood pushed back his chair and rose. "I think we'll have coffee on the pool terrace," he suggested. "It's a glorious starlit night, and I'm very proud of my new patio."

Outside, the dinner guests moved into different patterns. Lisette saw Don talking with her father, but she didn't join them. Instead, she listened to Kyle asking Mr. Hood's secretary whether she knew of a manuscript typist who was proficient in English. "I write in longhand," she explained, "but I need a typed draft before I can polish the text."

Miss Chieng Mai was pleasant but discouraging.

"You are asking for someone rather special," she told Kyle. "Girls of that caliber are usually already employed."

A few minutes later Kyle drifted back inside the house, and Lisette, prompted by unusual resolution, followed. She found Kyle standing before an elegant bronze Buddha with a towering headdress and braceleted ankles. Obviously thinking she was alone, Kyle very delicately reached out and traced the curve of the shoulders. Then, aware of Lisette's approach, she turned and spoke.

"Imagine the sheer joy of acquiring these wonderful things," she cried. "You know, Liz, there are women who would sell their souls for jewels, but I wouldn't give a fig for the biggest diamond on earth. If ever I were to be tempted—"

"Yes?"

Kyle shuddered slightly, then laughed. "I can't think what I was about to say."

Lisette, however, had not forgotten her own errand. "You were asking about a typist," she said. "I learned to type at the convent. I wonder if you could use me?"

Before Kyle could reply a sudden commotion made them both turn toward the dining room. The Englishwoman came stumbling over the threshold, coughing and spluttering in obvious distress, and on her heels came the tall Cambodian, with a handkerchief held to his face. The rest of the dinner guests crowded behind, pushing one another through the open glass doors unceremoniously. They seemed blinded, knocking against chairs and tables that were in the way.

Lisette saw that their eyes were streaming. A cloud of vapor surrounded them, wafted in from the terrace, and in a split second Lisette's own eyes began to smart. She saw Mr. Hood slam the sliding doors shut and turn the latch, then heard him call out angrily in Thai.

A servant came running with an opened box of tissues, which he passed out to the stricken guests. He was as polite and as imperturbable as ever, but his employer was obviously furious.

"What happened?" Kyle asked Miss Chieng Mai, who was the first to reach the salon. After wiping her eyes and blowing her nose, she choked out a reply. "Someone threw a tear-gas bomb over the garden wall."

A tear-gas bomb! Lisette knew that French police threw them to dispel rioters, but to have one thrown into a private patio was very strange indeed. Who could have done such a thing—and why?

Mr. Hood, who was walking about apologizing to his dinner guests, seemed to have hit on an easy solution. "A childish prank no doubt." He sighed. "But most regrettable."

Lisette went over to her father. "Are you all right, Papaul?"

But Alex didn't seem to hear her. "Prank, nothing," he said to Courtney Hood. "Thai kids can't get their hands on bombs like that. Make no mistake, somebody's got it in for you!"

VI

The return ride to the palace was easy and quick, because the streets had emptied. Don Hall sat in front with the driver, a bundle of clean clothes on his lap. "Who's minding camp while you're off cavorting with the idle rich?" Alex asked, as they neared the river.

"I've got a friend, one of the idle poor," replied Don over his shoulder. He told Kyle where he wanted to be let out, and Kyle translated his request to the driver. As Don said good-night he proposed Saturday for the sightseeing excursion on which he had invited Lisette. "Usually it's a busy morning on the *khlongs*."

Arrangements were made to meet at the main gate at six fifteen. "An ungodly hour," commented Kyle with a yawn, "but you'll find the sacrifice worth it, Liz." Don went off into the dark whistling cheerfully to himself, and the others drove on to the palace, where the aged gatekeeper, called Mr. Thanoo, had been given strict instructions to be on hand to admit them.

During the next three days life fell into a routine. Alex, up with the sun, prowled the palace complex taking outdoor shots while the morning light was good, then returned to the villa and worked in an improvised darkroom until lunchtime. Kyle stayed at her desk, surrounded by reference books, and covered page after page of lined yellow paper in longhand. Lisette explored the grounds, coming across her father in unlikely places, standing on a balustrade, astride the back of a stone elephant, leaning precariously from a balcony, even perched on a pagoda roof, trying to get a dramatic angle shot.

Kyle didn't take Lisette up on her offer to act as typist until she had exhausted Bangkok's English-speaking employment agencies. Finally, one afternoon, she said, "See if you can read my writing, Liz. Then try a page or two, one-inch margins, double-spaced."

Lisette was more than willing, as the middle of the day dragged for her. Furthermore, she found typing Kyle's text interesting, because she learned new things about the palace as she went along. She was quite unprepared, however, for Kyle's cry of appreciation. "Why, Liz, you're very good! There are only two typos on this whole page." Apparently she was very impressed by the proficiency of the nuns' teaching.

So Lisette found herself with a job—a paid job! She was to work three hours a day starting the following Monday. Saturday morning she told Don Hall about her new employment as they rode a series of crowded buses to the stop nearest the Oriental Hotel. Thinking of Philippe, she said, "It'll help pass the time."

Don paid for the launch tickets with Thai money Alex had given Lisette for the purpose. He was already so familiar with the unit of currency—called a *baht*—that he treated Thai coins as casually as if he had been reared with them.

Disdaining the sleek modern motorboats being loaded with groups of tourists, Don led Lisette to an awninged native craft with an outboard. Brown hands reached out to help her aboard. Smiling faces greeted her. The Thai boatmen were so hospitable that she pretended to be comfortable on the hard board seats.

Once filled to capacity, the boat left the dock, heading up the Chao Phya river for a mile or so, then cutting over to the west bank and entering a maze of busy canals.

Lisette wound a scarf around her head to keep her hair from blowing and put on a pair of dark sunglasses. She felt her curiosity was less conspicuous if the market people in sampans crowding close to the boat couldn't see her eyes.

The fragile skiffs were loaded with all kinds of produce. Heaps of oranges, limes, pineapples, and pomelos stood side by side with mounds of red and green peppers, lettuces, and tomatoes. One boatman sold flowers and plants, another carried baskets of peeping chicks and caged mynah birds, still another offered bolts of cheap cotton. From wooden platforms in front of waterside shops, hawkers held out pottery bowls for sale, while at the same time two monks edged their sampan toward an eager merchant, with their own bowls held forth.

"What are they doing?" Lisette asked Don. "Begging?"

"Sure. They've taken vows of poverty. Each morning they collect their day's food this way."

"But the people who help them are so poor themselves!" Lisette protested.

Don agreed. "Still, for those who feed them, it's a good way to reach Nirvana."

"Nirvana?"

"A state of grace. Perhaps you'd call it the Buddhist heaven."

At that moment the overheated outboard motor stalled, and the cluster of sampans crowded the launch closer to the muddy bank, near which Thai children darted about like fishes in the dark water. The boatman pulled the engine up and started to tinker with it unhurriedly, while Don and another young man went aft to look on.

Khlong-side shops had given way to a group of wooden houses with waterside gardens of dendrobium orchids, grown in handsome clay pots. On a porch built on stilts, so close to Lisette that she could have reached out and touched them, two men were arguing, quite oblivious to the confusion of canal traffic at their feet. One was too tall and thin for a Thai; the other was diminutive, with small hands and feet, smooth skin the color of caramel, and a

91

receding hairline. Yet he was the one who seemed to have the upper hand. Shaking his fist in the air angrily, he attracted the attention of the sampan hucksters, who seemed unused to seeing such violence on an ordinary market day.

Although Lisette could hear their voices quite plainly, she couldn't understand a word they said until suddenly the name of Courtney Hood reached her with startling clarity. She looked again and recognized the Cambodian with a mole on his cheek whom she had met at the dinner party. This morning, however, Foxy—as she mentally called him—had lost all his composure. His face was purple with rage, and he began shouting uncontrollably.

One of the launch's Thai passengers, who looked like an educated man, seemed embarrassed. As Foxy finally stopped shouting and turned away with a resigned shrug to walk up some steps into the house, the native tourist seemed relieved that the episode was over. "Not Thais," the man said to Lisette in broken English. "Is Cambodians, both."

Lisette smiled and nodded. "Very angry," she murmured.

"Liz, come look!" Attracted by a sampan vendor with a gibbon for sale, Don beckoned from the rear of the boat.

Lisette joined him, although the chattering creature on a chain interested her less than the altercation she had just witnessed. "Don, did you see those two men?"

"What men?"

"The ones who were shouting at each other, up there on that platform."

Don shook his head, without taking his eyes off the gibbon. "How much?" he asked the owner. Then he practised one of his few Thai phrases. *"Tao rai?"*

"Listen, Don!" Lisette tugged at the boy's arm, knowing he wasn't going to buy the little ape, but the flood of Thai bargaining he had provoked could not be stopped. "Don!" Lisette raised her own voice above the din. "Do you know who one of those men was? He was that Cambodian we met at Mr. Hood's!"

"Oh, come on!" Don said in disbelief and with little interest.

"Honestly!" Lisette insisted.

"If so, what of it?"

"He was talking about Mr. Hood."

"Well, that's allowable." Don grinned and scratched his peeling nose. "We seem to be talking about him too."

"But not in the same way. Those men were fighting. That's different. And even though he's a friend of your father's, you'll have to admit that Mr. Hood is sort of mysterious, with his beautiful house and beautiful secretary and his strange dealings and—"

"And the tear-gas bomb?"

Lisette nodded. She was remembering her father had thought it anything but a prank.

Don followed her back to their seats and sank down beside her. "Thailand's a mysterious country," he said, "but don't let your imagination run away with you. If we ever get out of this traffic jam, I'll take you to see the place where a man of *real* mystery lived."

An hour and a half later he led Lisette along a shady lane off Petchaburi Road to a tropical-garden setting for a traditional Thai structure of black teak.

Overhung by leafy trees and surrounded by flowering shrubs and plants, the place was a dim, cool oasis in the midst of the desert heat of Bangkok. "Jim Thompson built this from six old houses, and now it's a kind of museum in his memory," Don explained.

Jim Thompson again. "Who *was* Jim Thompson?" Lisette asked. Her father had forgotten his promise to tell her about him.

Such ignorance seemed to astonish Don. "Just about the most famous American who ever lived in Bangkok," he said. "He's the guy who put Thai silk on the map."

"Oh?" Lisette was unimpressed.

"Wake up, Liz! Jim Thompson was important—

very important. All along these *khlongs* there were silk farmers, poor people who knew how to raise silkworms and weave silk, but who didn't have a clue as to how to produce and sell the stuff in quantity. Thompson built factories. He created jobs. He sold Thai silk all over the world. And he made a fortune doing it."

Lisette glanced around the handsome covered terrace on which they were waiting for a guide to show them through the house. Obviously it had been the residence of a rich man.

"He put people to work at a time when work was scarce, my pop says," continued Don. "Then one day he walked out of this house and was never seen again."

Finally Lisette's attention was caught. "What happened?"

"Nobody knows. He simply disappeared."

"Did he have enemies?"

Don shrugged.

"But he couldn't just walk off the face of the earth. There must have been some clues."

Don shook his head, his ragged hair glinting in the splinters of sunlight slanting through the trees. "Not a clue. The most educated guess is that he might have been the victim of a political murder, but who knows? This is the mysterious East."

The guide took Lisette and Don through the rambling house, along with five elderly tourists. Adopting an almost reverential air, she described the paintings, porcelains, and statues that Jim Thompson had collected, but Lisette barely listened. She was thinking about the man himself.

Looking from a bedroom window into the black water of the *khlong,* where a naked child was floating a banana-leaf boat, she was swept by a feeling of threat. As she breathed the fragrance of jasmine mingled with the stench of stagnant water, the thought occurred to her that anything could happen here—anything at all! If a person made one misstep, he could disappear without a trace.

The moment the tour was over, Don hurried Lisette away. He announced that he was famished and knew a little place—very clean!—where they could have something to eat. Afterward they worked their way back toward the palace on a series of stifling buses. Then Don proposed that Lisette come take a look at his riverside camp.

Although curious, Lisette demurred. She had a feeling that her father might have expected her back much earlier—even for lunch. "Maybe some other time?"

"It won't take ten minutes. And it's cooler down by the river. You'll see." Not to be dissuaded, Don glanced at the sky and added, "I'll have you home long before it starts to rain."

Lisette allowed herself to be persuaded. The trees that bordered the river looked tall and shady, but if it was cooler under their arching branches she couldn't detect it. Half a dozen small tents, set higgledy-piggledy on a grassy bank, lay a few hundred yards away, and toward these Don gestured. "The Bangkok Biltmore. Expensive, but worth it."

"You mean you actually *live* here?"

"What's wrong with it?"

Everything, Lisette thought, as she came closer. The tents were ragged and dirty, as were the campers lolling on the rough brown grass. "Want to meet some of my friends?" asked Don with a grin.

"They're not your *friends*!" Lisette protested.

"Not really," Don admitted. "But they live here, same as I do. Most of them may be crazy, but they're not too bad."

The remark reminded Lisette of her father. Papaul was interested in people—people of all sorts, good and bad, rich and poor, amusing and dull. Apparently Don shared this propensity.

He nodded at a tall, thin boy with high cheekbones and sunken eyes, but he didn't stop to introduce her, for which Lisette was thankful. Yet she shot a second glance at the fellow, fascinated as she might have been by a cobra, because his appearance was thoroughly repulsive. Lank hair, parted in the middle, hung halfway down his back. Around his forehead was a beaded band, around his neck a string of cowrie shells, and on each hand he wore three big turquoise rings, which must have hampered him in his effort to mend a torn tent flap. From his tent pole waved a flag bearing a coiled rattlesnake ensign and a printed legend: *Don't Tread on Me.*

"That's Bobby," whispered Don, when they were well past. "He's spaced out."

Shuddering, Lisette wished she hadn't come. She couldn't help feeling sorry for the boy, although she knew her mother would be horrified by such an unpalatable scene. Even her easygoing father would be provoked at Don for bringing her here.

Yet she could find no easy way to escape. Don led her past an African boy wearing Indian pajamas, who was fast asleep on the ground, waved casually to a bearded youth tuning a guitar, and arrived at a grove of spindly trees that sheltered two tents set apart from the others.

Don pointed to the nearer one. "That's mine!"

The tent was so small that Lisette asked, "Don't your feet stick out when you go to bed?"

"I sleep outside, unless it's raining. Mostly, I use it as a place to stow my gear. Want to see inside?"

He sounded so much like a proud homeowner that Lisette couldn't refuse, and, indeed, the dim interior did look more orderly than she had expected. "My pop and I used to go camping in the Outback," Don told her. "He taught me to keep things squared away. It makes life easier."

As she straightened up, a boy with a shaved head, coming from a nearby tent, caught Lisette's attention. In contrast to the long-haired hippies, he looked especially peculiar, but his brown eyes were as friendly as a spaniel's. "Hi, Don," he said, "Who's the chick?"

"Lisette Paul," retorted Don. "And she's no chick. She's a friend of mine who just happens to be living at the palace."

"Oh, yeah?" The spaniel-eyed boy sounded skeptical.

"This is Spooky, who keeps an eye on my tent when I go out," explained Don. "He's resting up here until his hair grows."

"What happened to your hair?" ventured Lisette.

"Like this, I was in Singapore, see. How could I know they don't allow long hair in Singapore? So the police round up a bunch of us and haul us to the Orchard Road police station, where a guy with a razor almost scalps us. Very humiliating."

"I should think so," murmured Lisette.

"He's lucky he wasn't deported," said Don.

Spooky shrugged. "It wouldn't have mattered. I was ready to leave anyway." He turned from Lisette and spoke directly to Don. "Hey, Bobby's splitting next week, have you heard? He's moving on to Meshed. That's a city in Iran," he added for Lisette's benefit.

"Why Meshed?" asked Don.

"He says it's funky. It's loose. He wants me to go along."

"Take my advice and keep clear of Bobby and his tribe," advised Don quickly. "Come on, Liz. You've seen enough, haven't you?"

More than enough, Lisette could have replied. Instead, she merely nodded. Longing to get away, she hurried back past the tent where Bobby was now sitting cross-legged, rolling a wad of sticky brown stuff that looked like a plug of English toffee between his thumb and forefinger.

"What was that?" she whispered in distaste.

"Do you really want to know?"

"Otherwise I wouldn't have asked," Lisette replied with asperity.

"Opium," said Don flatly. "Bobby is bad news. He's into every kind of dope there is. And right now he's plotting some kind of rip-off. I wish I knew what it was."

VII

The main gate was closed when Lisette and Don reached the palace. Visiting hours were over and the courtyard was empty except for Alex, who was pacing up and down like a caged cheetah inside the iron grille.

"Where have you been?" he demanded, sounding

as indignant as a Victorian father. "I didn't expect you to be gone *all day!*"

Thus accosted, Don couldn't help but appear guilty. "I'm sorry, sir. We had lunch. Then, on the way back, I took Liz down to the river for a look at my camp."

"Without any thought that I might be getting worried?" Alex didn't expect the question to be answered. "Accidents happen on the *khlongs,* nasty accidents." He beckoned to Mr. Thanoo, who was standing out of sight against the inner wall. "You can unlock the gate now."

Lisette had to dogtrot to keep up with her father's quick pace as they walked toward the villa. "It never occurred to me that you'd be concerned, Papaul," she murmured breathlessly.

Alex was not to be placated. "It should have occurred to you," he snapped, stalking ahead. "After all, Bangkok isn't the safest place in the world!"

"You never told me that, Papaul."

"Well, I'm telling you now." Alex pulled up short while Mr. Thanoo opened the gate leading to the Inside. He looked at Lisette so sternly that she almost burst out laughing, yet at the same time she was touched.

Kyle was lying on a lounge chair in the garden, reading. "Here she is," said Alex indignantly, and waved a hand in Lisette's direction as though he had just rescued a recalcitrant puppy from imminent disaster. Then, without another glance in his daughter's direction, he stamped inside.

Kyle put down her book and regarded Lisette with a hint of amusement in her expression. "He loves you," she said softly. "He really loves you! I never dreamed he could get so upset."

"I was perfectly all right."

"Of course, you were." Kyle smiled at Lisette understandingly, almost as though they were conspirators protesting male domination. Then her attention returned to the book she had been reading, and Lisette went upstairs to bathe and change her clothes.

On the desk in her bedroom she found two letters, one from her mother and one from Philippe, addressed in the small, careful script learned by every French schoolboy. He was playing a lot of tennis. The family cat had just had five kittens. His sister was taking riding lessons. Brittany was as full of vacationists in July as it usually was in August. He missed her and hoped she was having a good time.

Dear Philippe, thought Lisette, although she found the letter vaguely disappointing. Everything at the seashore seemed unchanged, the summer days passing in the same relaxed fashion as usual, yet she no longer wished she was there.

Her mother's letter was longer and full of sensible advice. Lisette should be very careful of what she ate and drank—particularly careful to drink nothing but boiled water!—because Bangkok was undoubtedly full of disease. (If Maman could see the place where I had lunch, she'd be appalled, Lisette thought with a smile.) Never go out on the streets alone, her mother warned. I trust your father has provided a chaperone. (Don, a fine chaperone!) France and Maman's mode of living seemed infinitely restricting. I've changed, Lisette thought, in these few short weeks, but at home everything has stayed the same.

In France, she was cosseted and protected during these years when she was considered not yet a woman but no longer a child. Here her father and Kyle accepted her on her own terms. When she behaved in adult fashion, they treated her as an adult—until today.

Yet her father's behavior continued to warm Lisette's heart. He loved her, Kyle had said. He really loved her!

The afternoon rain came late, and the storm was brief, but on Sunday it showered off and on all day. Lisette thought of Don, huddling in his inadequate pup tent, and wondered whether he had yet learned what Bobby was up to. "Papaul, can you tell me what is meant by the term *rip-off*?" she asked.

"Ask me something easy," Alex suggested. "Suppose a couple of thieves rip off the owner of a jewelry store. They steal him blind, in other words."

"Steal him—blind?"

"That's another slang expression," said Alex. "Let's take one at a time." He hesitated a moment. "A rip-off is sort of a stunt, often a criminal stunt. Kyle, how would you define a rip-off?"

Kyle, who was mending a tear in a pair of denim pants, said, "You're doing beautifully. I'm sure Liz knows just as much as she did before she asked."

"You're a big help!"

Kyle smiled sweetly. "I'm not into current jargon the way you are, Alex. It's not my bag!"

Lisette knew Kyle was teasing, but she still found American slang daunting. It was about as intelligible as rhyming Cockney, a British type of speech her nanny had once tried to explain.

"Never mind, Papaul. It's not important."

Kyle raised an eyebrow. "That depends on who's being ripped off."

Alex stood up and stretched, turning his back on the conversation as he peered out of the open windows at the streaming rain. "I hope it stops by tomorrow," he muttered. "I've got a big morning's work mapped out."

Monday morning, as it turned out, was quite clear.

The rain-washed air was sparkling, and Lisette, awakening early, decided to join her father on his morning picture-taking expedition.

By now the palace grounds were becoming so familiar that the pair knew several shortcuts to the irregular square where the Temple of the Emerald Buddha was enclosed by galleries. Constructed of whitewashed brick and roofed with red tiles, the walls were pierced by a number of heavy wooden doors. Avoiding some fresh whitewash, Alex pushed open one of these doors with the case of his Hasselblad, a viewing camera he used for special color shots. Carrying a couple of tripods, Lisette inched through after him and came out to the quiet terrace peopled only by enormous fantastic statues and the equally fantastic collection of chapels, halls, and pavilions that surrounded the Buddha's shrine.

Now was the loveliest time of day, when she and her father had the place to themselves, before the tourists arrived. This morning was picture perfect. A few fat white clouds made a backdrop for nine conical towers standing in a row on the eastern side of the stone platform. Alex whistled. "Beautiful!"

Working rapidly, he seized the larger tripod and set up his camera. "If I can just catch those clouds!"

Lisette had learned enough about her father's techniques to understand why he was in a hurry. The flat blue of the usual morning sky was far less dramatic than the setting offered today. Each spire was covered with glazed tiles, but no two were alike, she noticed. Then she remembered Kyle's remark that the colors had been selected to correspond with the colors of the nine planets comprising the universe of King Rama I. Even Lisette's untrained eye could see that the spires wouldn't prove easy to photograph. They tended to bunch together from almost every angle, leading Alex from place to place, trying to find a spot from which they would appear as separate entities.

He took half a dozen shots, but kept shaking his head. "They look like a bunch of syringes," he complained to Kyle, when she came by on her way to the library situated in a corner of the temple courtyard. "Take a look through this lens."

Kyle stooped, considered the composition for several seconds, then nodded. "Quills stuck upright in a bed of sand."

Alex tugged at his beard unhappily. "This guy Rama must have had it in for photographers. The clouds have moved out of range anyway. I'll try to get a better angle some other day."

"Come along with me, Liz," Kyle suggested. "You've never been inside the library, and there are some rather wonderful cabinets I'd like you to see."

107

Lisette followed along willingly and discovered that Rama I was also responsible for some lacquered teak bookcases inlaid with mother-of-pearl. "He must have been a busy king," she remarked. While Kyle seated herself at a table and opened the volume she had come to consult, Lisette wandered around the big room, which smelled of wax and old leather, then went back to stand in the doorway to try to see what her father was doing now.

Alex was no longer in sight. The courtyard was empty except for two guards unlocking the doors of the temple and a couple of sweepers brushing down the steps. Birds twittered from the gallery roof, and myriads of bells tinkled softly in the slightest breeze. It was a scene of perfect peace, so why, Lisette wondered, did she still feel uneasy? Two days ago there might have been cause for alarm, but now the black water of the *khlongs* was far away and the campers outside the palace walls posed no threat here.

Or did they?

Bobby was planning a rip-off, and, according to Don, Bobby was bad news.

An elderly guard carrying a bunch of keys shuffled by with bent shoulders, recognized Lisette, and nodded with an almost toothless smile. *"Sawat dee,"* Lisette called, proud to be able to say good morning in Thai.

"Sawat dee," the old man returned, and Lisette felt pleased by his cordiality. Recently there had been a change in attitude of the palace servitors. They had learned to accept the presence of the foreigners who were staying on the Inside and spoke to them as if—temporarily, at least—they belonged.

Restless, because Kyle was taking longer than she had expected, Lisette wandered back inside. She found Kyle making notes on a scratch pad. "Listen to this!" Kyle said, looking up. "I've found some old laws relating to the profanation of idols." She read aloud:

"If a thief steal an image of Buddha, and use various devices for removing its ornaments, such as washing or smelting, let him be put into a furnace and treated in exactly the same way as he treated the image, and thus pay for his wickedness.

"That's Section Forty-eight of the Siamese civil code. The next section becomes even more barbaric!

"If any thief strip a Buddha image of its gold or gilding, let him be taken to a public square and a red-hot iron rubbed over him until he is stripped of his skin, as he stripped the image of gold,

109

and thus pay for his crime. If a thief scratch the gold from a Buddha image, pagoda, or temple, or sacred tree, let his fingers be cut off."

In spite of herself, Lisette shivered. "They don't really do that, do they? I mean, not today?"

"I shouldn't think so," Kyle replied quickly, "but it gives one pause."

Lisette nodded, her uneasiness increased. "Will you be here much longer?" she asked.

"Five or ten minutes."

"I think I'll walk over to the Temple and see if Papaul is working inside. Will you stop by for me?"

"Gladly. And as soon as we're back at the house, I'll get you started at the typewriter," Kyle suggested, as she turned another page of the book.

Alex wasn't in the Temple when Lisette arrived, but the first group of tourists were taking off their shoes on the steps. Inside, the Emerald Buddha gazed down from his dimly lighted throne with three diamond eyes—the third in the middle of his forehead. His air of imperturbability was so awesome that the tourists automatically lowered their voices as they entered, and their feet made no sound on the tiled floor.

Lisette stood at the back, watching. By now she knew the routine. The guide would explain that this temple was unique in Thailand, because it contained articles of real value. He would let the visitors feast their eyes on the Emerald Buddha for a few minutes, then tell them something of its history. After a tour of the chapel, he would take them behind the altar to see the ladder climbed by the ruling monarch when he changed the Buddha's clothes. Finally he would show them a square table containing seven solid gold Buddha images whose hands glittered with sapphire, emerald, and ruby rings. Each hand pointed upward toward the little jade god, seated on a golden throne half hidden in the shadows, the unique Emerald Buddha, venerated above any other in the land.

There was the sound of a scuffle at the entrance. Lisette, staying close to the exit door so that she wouldn't miss Kyle, turned in time to see Bobby lurch into the chapel on the heels of Don Hall.

Don apparently became aware of his presence at almost the same moment. He put a finger to his lips with a warning "Sh!" which Bobby ignored. With his thumbs tucked into the pockets of his ragged jeans, he stopped, blinking in the dim interior, and asked loudly, "Hey, Don boy, what brings you here?"

Don didn't reply, yet he didn't move away from Bobby. The tour group followed their guide toward the altar, giving the barefoot newcomers a wide berth. Lisette, watching from the shadows, realized

111

the tourists put Don in the same category as Bobby. She wasn't especially surprised, since Don looked almost as disreputable.

In a patient voice, Don said, "Look, Bobby, this is a holy place. Let's go somewhere else. How about it?"

Bobby shook his head. He swung a long arm across Don's shoulders and leaned against him, breathing heavily. With glazed eyes he peered up at the distant Buddha. Then, looking out of touch with reality, he removed his arm from Don's shoulders and started uncertainly toward the exit door, passing Lisette without apparently seeing her.

An instant later Lisette found Kyle at her side. "Good Lord, who was that creature?"

"A bloke who hangs out down by the river," replied Don, waiving the formality of a greeting. "I'd better stay with him. He's in bad shape."

VIII

"Your young friend keeps strange company," said Kyle to Lisette in a tone of disgust as they walked down the broad steps that led from the temple terrace.

"I think Don was just trying to be helpful," Lisette replied defensively.

"Helpful? That character is on LSD or hashish or something."

"Opium," said Lisette, to Kyle's astonishment.

"You mean you *know* him?"

"Not really, but I know something about him. His name is Bobby, and he's one of the hippies who have pitched their tents near Don's."

"Don looked pretty scroungy himself this morning," Kyle said caustically.

Instinctively protective of her own generation, Lisette started to protest. She broke off, however, as she saw her father in the distance, standing near his camera, which was set up in the shade of a gallery affording a good view of a wooden bell tower. He was talking to a man and woman who looked vaguely familiar: the man plump, middle-aged, and bald; the younger woman poured into a tight cotton dress. The sight jogged Lisette's memory. The Dillons, of course. They must have finished their business in Singapore.

"Papaul's talking to some people we met on the plane," Lisette told Kyle. "Do you want to meet them?"

After a quick glance in the Dillons' direction, Kyle said in an undertone, "Not very much."

Lisette stifled a giggle, because Kyle had spoken too late. Alex had seen them and was beckoning. He introduced his colleague with some ceremony and said, "Professor Goodfellow is writing the text of the book I'm working on."

"Professor!" Mr. Dillon's shrewd little eyes traveled from Kyle's fair hair, bleached lighter than ever by the Bangkok sun, to the painted toenails peeping from her sandals and back up again. "You've got to be kidding!" he said.

Kyle, knowing that the remark was intended as a compliment, accepted it with more grace than Lisette could possibly have mustered. In an effort to make small talk, she asked, "You're enjoying the palace, I hope?"

"We *always* enjoy the palace," said Mr. Dillon, correcting the inference that he and his wife might be there for the first time. "We've come to pay a visit to our Buddha, just as we always do."

"*Your* Buddha?"

Mrs. Dillon giggled. "Ralph always refers to it as *our* Buddha. He positively adores it. I think he would give a million dollars to be able to tuck it under his arm and take it home."

"Fat chance," muttered Mr. Dillon, who seemed embarrassed. "It's a national treasure, cookie. You know that."

"You're speaking of the Emerald Buddha?" Kyle asked.

"What else?"

"Such acquisitiveness embarrasses me," Kyle confessed to Lisette after they had walked on. "Yet I understand the desire to own a great piece of art. You know the old Chinese proverb, that one picture

115

is worth more than ten thousand words." She shrugged graphically. "In Mr. Dillon's mind one statue apparently ranks even higher."

Back at the villa, Lisette forgot all about the Dillons. She worked for the rest of the morning on Kyle's text, typing rather slowly but with the careful accuracy the nuns had insisted upon. Alex came in as soon as the sun climbed too high to cast interesting shadows, and at noon, to Lisette's surprise, the Dillons reappeared.

Escorted by Mr. Thanoo, who had apparently been bribed to open the gate and bring them to the villa, they were rather boisterous. "My little lady is just as thirsty as can be, and since the sun is over the yardarm we thought we might persuade you to buy us a drink," Lisette heard Mr. Dillon shout.

That'll teach you, Papaul, she thought to herself. Taking up with strangers doesn't always work out well.

Alex, however, seemed unperturbed. He mixed aperitifs with easy hospitality and questioned the Dillons on their Singapore purchases.

This seemed rather forward to Lisette, but the Dillons appeared delighted to talk about the finds they had made. In particular, they were pleased with a pair of biscuit-colored porcelain elephants made for the Chinese export trade in the eighteenth century.

"They're in mint condition," said Mr. Dillon proudly.

"And Ralph thought they were a real good buy," added his wife. "They only cost ten thousand dollars."

"Cookie, you mustn't talk about price," Mr. Dillon objected.

Pouting at the reprimand, Mrs. Dillon said, "You do."

"Only to dealers. Which reminds me, Courtney Hood is having dinner with us tonight." Mr. Dillon swept the group with his eyes. "We'd be mighty pleased to have you join us."

Lisette hoped her father would make an excuse or that Kyle would find a polite way to refuse, but instead the two, unable to consult privately, hesitated a moment too long.

"Capital!" cried Mr. Dillon, as though their acceptance was assured. He fixed his glance on Lisette and added, "Tell you what! So that this young lady won't be bored, we'll take you to a place that features traditional Thai dancing."

After the Dillons left, Kyle moaned to Alex, "Why did you?"

Alex retorted, "Why didn't *you*?" Then they both laughed. "OK, so we're in for it. Anyway, maybe we need another evening out."

As it happened, Lisette enjoyed the Thai dancing.

Beautiful girls in exquisite costumes performed the parts of both male and female participants as the music described their actions—courtship, mirth, anger, despair. Between acts the adults talked art, and once more Mr. Hood tried to persuade Alex to photograph his collection.

"Let's leave it at this," Lisette's father at last proposed, obviously feeling more secure on the neutral ground of the restaurant than he had in Courtney Hood's lavish home. "If I can wangle a free weekend before I go back to the States, I'll give you a ring."

"Were you just putting him off, Papaul?" Lisette asked on the way home.

Alex made a gesture of uncertainty. "I'm not sure."

The next morning he was up and off with his cameras before Lisette awakened. She dawdled over breakfast, then pushed aside her tray and lay back on the pillows thinking about the Thai dancing girls with their long artificial fingernails and their studied movements. What sort of lives, she wondered, did they live when they weren't working? Were some of them married perhaps? Or were they in school?

Eventually she got up, bathed, and put on her coolest shift. From the window she could see that again there were cumulus clouds in the sky, so probably her father had returned to the task of trying to capture the nine conical towers on color film.

118

Looking up from her desk when Lisette came downstairs, Kyle confirmed the notion. "He's going to try a new approach and get people in the picture. Why don't you wander over and see how he's making out, Liz, before it gets too hot?"

Lisette glanced at the salon clock. She usually started her secretarial work at eleven, and it was not yet ten. "All right," she said, as she prepared to leave the house. "I'll be back in about an hour."

Kyle murmured, "Mmm" without glancing up. We've grown accustomed to one another, Lisette thought, as she was let through the gate to the Outside by Mr. Thanoo. It was a comfortable relationship, easier in many ways than the one she had with her father.

Alex she still found unpredictable. Last night he had been merry and laughing, full of sallies that kept the Dillons amused. In contrast, Mr. Hood had seemed preoccupied, taking little part in the conversation, in spite of the fact that his host was an enormously wealthy client, certainly worth cultivating.

At the end of the evening he had hurried off with only perfunctory thanks, his behavior in such strong contrast to his courtly manners of a few evenings before that Lisette kept wondering what had distracted him.

There was very little chance of finding out. Mr. Hood's affairs seemed almost as enigmatic as those of the Cambodian who had been his dinner guest. Twice during dinner she had made an attempt to tell Mr. Hood about her encounter on the *khlong,* but each time she had been interrupted by Mrs. Dillon, who displayed remarkably little sensitivity.

This morning Lisette noticed that tourists were already lined up outside the enormous gate through which richly caparisoned elephants had once carried reigning monarchs. A few authorized guides waited inside, their eyes darting past people in organized groups to those traveling independently. Two saffron-robed monks, food-filled begging bowls in hand, walked solemnly from an inner courtyard and waited for the gatekeeper to let them out. A pair of painters pushed a heavy barrow loaded with a big vat of whitewash and some cans of colored paint through an archway. They then headed across the big quadrangle where souvenir sellers were putting the finishing touches on their awninged stands.

Lisette hurried after the sweating painters, eager to get ahead of the first wave of tourists. Running past the creaking barrow and up the steps to the temple terrace, she looked around but couldn't see her father.

"Hey, Liz! I'm up here."

Alex spoke from the balcony of a wooden pagoda. He leaned over the railing and beckoned. "There's an inside stairway you can climb, if the guard understood my sign language and left it unlocked."

The door *had* been left ajar, so Lisette ran up the creaking steps quickly, glad to be out of the sun. From this height the temple compound took on a different aspect. She was above the roofs of some of the small pavilions and on a level with the heads of the demon guardians. The tall towers her father wanted to photograph, however, still stretched above.

"I need people in the picture," said Alex at once. "Is the main gate open yet?"

"It should be," said Lisette. "There was quite a crowd waiting when I went past."

"Good." Alex swung the big camera a little to the left and adjusted his focus. He wore a smaller Nikon on a strap around his neck. Although Lisette seldom saw him use it, he seemed to regard this camera as a sort of talisman, left over from his newspaper days.

Along the side of the Temple of the Emerald Buddha came the painters, pushing and shoving their barrow to a position near the corner of the building out of the path of traffic and close to the entrance doors. One man immediately began to stir a can of red paint, and another set a short ladder against a pillar supporting an open pavilion and started to

121

climb toward the sloping, intricately decorated eaves.

From a distance came a stream of tourists—two large busloads, Lisette figured, separated into the usual French-, German-, and English-speaking groups. A few couples came behind at a more leisurely pace, talking with their privately hired guides, and a slight, small-boned, shaven-headed monk in the traditional yellow robe wheeled a companion monk in a carriage that looked like a bicycle rickshaw without the bicycle.

Monks were a common sight in this holiest of Bangkok's holy places. Lisette glanced at them briefly, knowing that they were undoubtedly headed toward the Temple of the Emerald Buddha, the doors of which were out of sight around the corner from where she stood. The great Temple, or great *bot,* as the guides always called it, was saved as the crowning point of the tour. First the tourists were led along the side wall toward the nine glistening towers.

There they paused, gazing upward through sunglasses, or from under the shelter of broad-brimmed hats, at the creations of a king who had been dead for nearly two hundred years. In a crouching position from behind his camera, Alex said, "That's the stuff!"

He was so intent on his picture taking that he didn't see another group of visitors approaching, but Lisette was aware of them the moment they came into view. They were a troop of the campers, and in a few seconds they swarmed up the terrace steps with Bobby at their head. He carried, with easily recognizable insolence, the flag Lisette had seen on his tent pole. This morning the rattlesnake's coils seemed actually to move in the sunlight, and the forked tongue flickered menacingly from the open mouth.

Lisette gave a slight gasp. Were they heading for the Temple of the Emerald Buddha? Could she get there in time to warn the guards? She was certain Bobby and his friends were contemplating some dangerous prank!

While she hesitated they marched into the range of her father's camera. Thinking only of his spoiled composition, Alex straightened up with a groan. "Those confounded kids! Who let that rabble in here?"

Lisette could have made a guess. They had infiltrated the palace compound one or two at a time, lulling the gatekeeper, unaware that they constituted a gang, into accepting their ticket money.

Bobby stopped, surrounded by his cohorts, as the tour guides began to move their groups on toward the model of the Angkor Wat. He was looking up at the golden spire of one of the towers while his companions playfully nudged and shoved him.

Alex came to stand at the railing of the balcony. "What do you suppose they're up to?" He tugged at his beard and added, "They're a mean-looking bunch."

They were indeed! Lisette recognized the black boy, still wearing his Indian pajamas, and the bearded guitarist. Spooky would have been easy to pick out, but there were no shaven heads.

And where was Don? Had he given up his role as Bobby's duenna? Lisette hoped so. Sincerely she hoped so! If her father discovered the Australian boy mixed up in this fracas he'd be less than amused.

Meanwhile, Bobby bent down and seemed to be rolling up his pant legs. The flag disappeared to emerge once more as he straightened. Oddly enough, he was grasping its stick in his teeth.

For an instant Lisette's eyes were caught by a hint of movement on the terrace steps. Kyle was walking toward the Temple of the Emerald Buddha, so self-absorbed that she was unaware of the commotion at the far side. Apparently heading for the entrance door, she quickly passed out of sight.

Then Bobby, with a raucous war whoop, leaped onto the platform of the nearest tower and began climbing its base with the agility of a monkey.

Alex groaned. "Good grief, doesn't that crazy kid realize those towers are sacred to the Thais? He's defiling—" Then he broke off as Lisette grasped his arm. "Oh, no! I don't believe it."

Bobby had reached the top of the stupa where religious relics lay buried. He paused imperceptibly to look up at the tall spire, then started to climb it, grabbing at the rough, inlaid surface with his bare hands and feet.

The tourists abandoned their march toward the Angkor Wat model and crowded back to watch. Bobby's companions cheered as he inched slowly upward. An elderly guard hurried around from the front of the Temple, and Alex cried, "Hey, what a picture story!" He unsnapped the case of his Nikon with the quick reaction of a former newspaperman.

Lisette stood watching as the crowd swelled. The two painters abandoned their touch-up work on the little pavilion and joined the throng, while the palace guard ran frantically to and fro, apparently unable to decide where his duty lay.

Alex didn't speak. He was busy taking exposures as rapidly as the camera would advance the film. Meanwhile, Lisette couldn't take her eyes from the climbing figure. Halfway up the spire now, Bobby was beyond the point where anyone could stop him, and he didn't seem to realize that his hands and feet had begun to bleed.

Suddenly Lisette was swept by a feeling of pity

125

that constricted her throat and made her clench her fists. That the poor boy could be so impervious to pain wasn't heroic; it was tragic. He needed help. He needed it desperately, but no one could reach him now.

As the cone narrowed toward the tip the going became easier. Bobby could actually grasp the spire in his arms as he neared the top. Again his companions cheered, not seeming to care that the noise brought two palace policemen running. They stood at the fringe of the crowd of spectators, shouting futile orders and looking upward, as helpless as anyone else.

Alex pointed his camera downward and caught a shot of them. Then he trained it on the overwrought guard, who was still racing back and forth on the verge of the crowd. He shouted something indistinguishable to the two policemen, then pulled up short and began to wring his hands.

At this point Kyle appeared around the corner of the Temple, almost bumping into the barrow filled with paint and whitewash. Like everyone else, she was looking up, and Lisette saw her stop in alarm and clap a hand to her mouth.

Bobby was very close to the top now. He got a knee grip on the cone and reached into his hip pocket with one hand, pulling out a length of twine. Finally

Lisette realized what the caper was all about. "He's going to tie the flag to the spire!" she said.

"The damn fool," growled Alex, but he brought his camera up again to catch the action.

Taking the flag from his teeth with the hand that held the twine, Bobby reached upward as a strange quiet settled on his audience. Lisette's knuckles were white where they grasped the balcony rail, and her father was watching, camera at the ready, for the boy's next move.

Bobby needed two hands to tie the knot that would secure the flag. He adjusted his knee grip and pushed his chest against the inlaid stone. Then, as he reached upward, he began to slip, and before he could catch himself he came hurtling down. As he fell he screamed like a wild animal.

With a prolonged "Aaah" of horror the spectators recoiled, stumbling back against one another in their rush to get out of the way. Lisette didn't see Bobby's body hit the ground, because she had covered her eyes. When she looked again, the police had taken charge. One was trying to hold the crowd back, and the other was kneeling beside the prostrate boy.

Alex flicked the camera strap over his head and handed the Nikon to Lisette. "Stay here," he ordered, and was gone, racing down the creaking stairs two steps at a time. He sprinted across the terrace, twisting in and out between sculptures and people as if he were running an obstacle course, passed Kyle without a glance, but was brought up short by the policeman, who didn't intend to let anyone—not even an American who lived inside the palace—escape his vigilance.

The distraught guard turned back once more to the Buddha's chapel that he was supposed to be protecting, just as Lisette heard her father shout, "Is there a doctor among you? A doctor?"

"Bitte sprechen Sie Deutsch," a man said.

Kyle came to Alex's rescue. *"Ein Mediziner?"*

A florid, clean-shaven man pushed his way forward, walked to the foot of the monument, and eased himself to his knees at Bobby's side. In less than a minute he got to his feet and turned to face the waiting throng.

Gravely he shook his head.

From somewhere in the crowd, as though acting in response to a signal, Don Hall emerged. He shook off the policeman's restraining hand and crossed the open space in front of the tower to pick up Bobby's fallen flag. Then, very solemnly, he walked over to the body and placed the cloth gently over the up-turned face. From where she stood on the balcony Lisette could read the legend plainly. *Don't Tread on Me.*

At that very instant, from the Temple of the Emerald Buddha, came the deep-pitched, sepulchral sound of a giant gong.

Boom. Boom. Boom.

⁋IX

Boom. Boom.

Reverberating through all the palace courtyards, the great gong seemed to be clanging a warning rather than sounding a knell. Lisette knew it was beaten only for royal ceremonies. Could one of Bobby's friends have gone berserk?

From her grandstand position she followed the next sequence of the drama with the detachment of a person watching a motion picture too strange to be believable. From every direction armed palace policemen came running, converging upon the crowd and herding everyone toward the covered arcade that enclosed the temple site.

Escaping just in time, Alex came bounding up the pagoda steps and quickly packed up his Hasselblad, then extracted the exposed film from the Nikon and wrapped it hastily in foil. "Keep this safe somewhere," he told Lisette, as he handed it to her. "And let's get out of here."

Boom. Boom. Boom. At last the sonorous clang stopped. The echoes, bouncing off the surrounding buildings, gradually died away.

"What's happening, Papaul? It isn't because Bobby—"

Alex shook his head, then admitted, "I don't know what's going on, but I don't think it would be smart to be found in the thick of things."

Apparently he had hopes of reaching the villa by a circuitous route that would avoid a confrontation with the police, but the moment he and Lisette reached the bottom of the steps they were spotted. Although separated from the rest, they were hurried along until they reached the gallery. As they passed the Temple Lisette noticed that the tall doors to the chapel were tightly closed.

A siren's wail split the middle distance. Soon an ambulance pulled up at the bottom of the terrace steps. Two white-clad Thais emerged, pulled a stretcher from the back, and followed one of the policemen toward the spot, out of sight around the corner of the Temple, where Bobby's body lay.

In a few minutes the hospital crew was back again, bent now under the weight of a form covered with a white sheet. For the first time Lisette came to grips with the fact that she had witnessed a tragedy, that she had covered her eyes too late to avoid seeing a young man start to fall to his death.

A chill touched her shoulders, and she shivered slightly, keeping close to her father as the tour guides interpreted the police chief's order to form a double line.

"Queue up," called a British voice. "They want us to queue up, Mabel."

Still in a state of shock, the tourists huddled together, resisting the efforts of the police to march them off somewhere. The campers were much more cooperative. Frightened by the possible retribution in store for them, they had turned as meek as lambs.

Up ahead, Lisette could see Kyle's bright hair. Apparently she was trying to persuade a recalcitrant

French couple that things would be easier for everyone if they would calm down and do as they were told. Finally the double line was formed, and the oddly assorted company started off, campers in front and the tourists bringing up the rear.

Plainly, they were being led toward the main gate, and on the way a number of stragglers were picked up, including the souvenir merchants, the soft-drink vendors, and the food sellers, who were unceremoniously ordered away from their stands without being given a chance to pack their wares. The legless man who sold rubbings was pushed into line on his cart. The watercolorist tucked his paintings under his arm and found a place near Lisette and her father. A bevy of cleaning women, crossing the big square with buckets and brooms, were faced about and attached to the end of the line. Everyone—even a stray dog that had slipped through the palace gate— was regarded suspiciously by the police.

By now the sun was high in the sky. The pavement's heat struck through Lisette's thin-soled shoes and her dress clung to her perspiring back. The handkerchief she carried was soaking wet, so she stuffed it into the pocket of her shift on top of her father's film and wiped her hands on her sides.

The foreign tourists looked as miserable as Lisette felt. Only those wearing straw hats could endure the midday heat of Bangkok. Yet the police were relentless. They herded the campers to one side and stopped the double line in front of the main gate. There a folding table had been set up. Behind it stood a young Thai boy holding an umbrella over the head of a uniformed official. Two policemen were stationed just inside the gate with revolvers drawn. They looked fierce and threatening to Lisette.

At her side, Alex tried to keep his big camera case in the scanty shade thrown by his body. "Film won't tolerate this kind of heat," he muttered unhappily.

Lisette's thoughts were off on a different tack. Could it be, she wondered, that the desecration of a sacred tower would cause such a violent reaction? The blasphemer was dead. Why must everyone be searched?

Quite obviously a full-scale investigation was taking place. One by one the tourists were brought up to stand in front of the man at the improvised desk. They were made to present their passports, open any bags they were carrying, then hand over their cameras, from which the film was extracted, sealed, and tossed into a box under the table.

Seeing this routine, Alex groaned.

"They won't take yours, Papaul," Lisette predicted comfortingly. "After all, we live here."

"Want to make a bet?"

"What could they want the film for, anyway?" Lisette wondered aloud.

"Beats me." Alex leaned close to Lisette's ear. "Try to hang on to that roll from the Nikon," he whispered. "Where have you got it?"

"In my pocket," Lisette whispered back.

"Better find a safer place."

Lisette thought for a minute, then felt in her pocket and wadded the damp handkerchief around the tinfoil-covered film. Reaching casually under the neckline of her sleeveless dress as if she were adjusting a shoulder strap, she inconspicuously tucked the handkerchief and film into her bra.

Alex grinned. "Good girl."

Lisette smiled back. "Save your compliments," she advised in a fair imitation of her father's speech. "We're not home free yet."

Off to the right, a new contingent of police was surrounding the campers. Their chief barked some unintelligible Thai orders, but the boys got the message. Spiritlessly, they marched back toward the interior compound once more.

"Wonder what they're doing? Making them revisit the scene of the crime?" Alex asked, as they disappeared.

"Maybe they're putting them in jail. There is a

place here, you know, where they used to hold criminals." Lisette was repeating information she had gleaned from Kyle.

"Those boys aren't criminals," Alex replied, as he inched forward in the slow-moving line. "The only one they could possibly consider a criminal is dead."

"It's all very strange, isn't it?" murmured Lisette.

"Too darned strange." There was a puzzled, apprehensive expression in Alex's blue eyes.

A plump, motherly woman in sensible oxfords and stockings, who was moving along just ahead of Lisette, suddenly leaned on her husband's arm and said, "I think I'm going to faint."

"You can't!" cried her husband, but Alex knew better.

"Get on your knees," he said. "Put your head down. There!"

The woman, who was streaming with perspiration, recovered slowly. "I've got to get out of here," she said. "Can't anybody do anything?"

Alex tried to get one of the tour guides to speak to the police, but the effort was futile. The Thais were following orders as they had been trained to do. Looking after a fainting woman was not a part of guard duty.

At a slow crawl, the inspection went on. Up ahead,

the monk pushing his companion in the clumsy wheelchair came abreast of the examiner and spoke to him in a soft, conciliatory manner, but if he expected to get off lightly he was wrong. A policeman ran his hands over the monk's yellow robe and felt around the legs of the cripple, who turned his head with a pained expression on his face. He had a mole on his cheek, Lisette noticed, reminding her of the Cambodian at Mr. Hood's dinner party. She wondered where that gentleman was right now—still at the house on the *khlong?*

Lisette could see Kyle step up to the table. The official, who apparently spoke English, said "Passport" for the fiftieth time.

"I haven't got it with me," returned Kyle in a clear, carrying voice. "It's back at the villa, on the Inside. We live here, you see. We're guests of the king."

"We?" Apparently the official knew nothing about the temporary residents.

Kyle indicated Lisette and her father by standing on tiptoe and pointing. "Miss Lisette and Mr. Alexander Paul."

"We haven't got our passports either," Alex called.

The official tapped his forehead with the heel of his hand. "Come up here," he ordered. "The two of you."

Lisette started forward, and Alex picked up his camera case and followed. The minute he reached the table the interviewer said, "Open that up."

"It's just my camera. I'm working here, taking pictures of the palace for a book. Don't you understand?"

The man looked totally uninterested. "Open up," he repeated, and glared at Alex while he unsnapped the locks.

Very deliberately the official took out the camera and extracted the film, then searched around in the case and confiscated an unexposed roll. Intermittently he eyed Alex balefully, as though he suspected him of treachery or worse.

The snakelike line of tourists was fidgeting impatiently. Lisette could hear them grumbling and wondered how the woman who had almost fainted was managing. Kyle caught her eye and shrugged ever so slightly, indicating that she knew no more than Lisette about what was going on.

"Turn out your pockets," said the official to Alex.

Lisette watched her father pull out a pencil stub, a rumpled handkerchief, a half-eaten pack of Lifesavers, and a handful of Thai coins.

"No more film?"

"No more."

The man turned to Lisette. "Handbag?"

139

She shook her head and spread her empty hands. "What have you got in your pocket?"

"Nothing." Lisette showed him.

The official looked her up and down, then turned back to Kyle. "I will send a policeman with you. Please see that he returns quickly with all three passports. And," he added as the trio turned away, "stay in the villa until further notice. That is an order."

"Aye, aye, Captain Bligh," murmured Alex under his breath.

Because of the presence of the policeman, who might have a schoolbook understanding of English, none of the three spoke as they walked to the gate leading to the Inside. Mr. Thanoo seemed relieved to see them, although he greeted them soberly, with no trace of his usual welcoming, nearly toothless smile.

Turning over the passports took only a few minutes. Kyle insisted that the policeman sign receipts for all three. "You can't be too careful in a situation like this," she said.

"Just what is the situation? Clue me in," suggested Alex.

"You know as much as I do," Kyle replied.

"Come on, be a sport and give an educated guess!"

"All right. It's only a guess, but I don't think the gang's stunt—or even the boy's death—is the reason for what's going on. I keep remembering a time at the museum when a small Rembrandt was stolen. Alarms rang all over the place, and every visitor was carefully searched on his way out."

"So the gong was like an alarm?" asked Lisette, as she removed her damp handkerchief from the roll of film and handed it to her father.

Kyle nodded. "I think something was stolen, something valuable."

"By one of Bobby's crowd?"

"Not necessarily," said Kyle.

"But it figures," broke in Alex. "One kid creates a diversion so another can nab the loot."

"I wish you'd talk decent English, Alex," Kyle said rather testily. "Liz will go back to France talking like a character in a Grade-B thriller."

Alex bounced the roll of film in the palm of his hand. "She's been acting like one. Do you know where she managed to hide this?"

"Papaul!" objected Lisette, flushing.

Alex laughed and put an arm around his daughter's shoulder, hugging her appreciatively. "You were very quick-witted, Liz," he said, without pursuing the subject. "If I'm lucky, I'll have a story I can sell to a picture magazine!" He glanced at his watch and added, "As a matter of fact, I think I'll get this into a tank of developer right now."

As soon as she and Kyle were alone, Lisette asked, "What do you think was stolen?"

"I haven't the faintest idea. And remember, Liz, this was only a guessing game."

Yet Lisette couldn't put the notion out of her mind. As she went dutifully to the typewriter she kept considering the possibility that one of the hippies —or even one of the tourists—had seized the opportunity to filch—what?

An emerald ring from the finger of a gold Buddha? A jewel-studded candlestick? One of the rare and precious gold vessels used for religious services? Near the base of the Temple altar were glass-fronted cases containing the expensive gifts of wealthy noblemen wishing to honor the Emerald Buddha. Might the thief have coveted one of them?

Lisette was still pondering the probabilities when lunch was announced by the Thai maid who always served them. Today she was unusually solemn. As she passed the plates she didn't giggle once. Along with everyone else, Lisette realized, the girl must have heard the echoing gong, must have recognized at once that something strange and frightening had happened. But if she knew what that something was, she didn't intend to share the secret with the foreigners.

Kyle and Alex cooperated in keeping the luncheon

conversation general, and Lisette fell in with their plan. They all pretended that this day was like any other, but they knew better. Virtual prisoners in the villa, they could no longer move freely around the palace grounds.

"Since we seem to be campused," said Kyle with intentional ambiguity, "how do you plan, Alex, to get your news pictures out?" They had returned to the salon, but nevertheless she spoke softly to guard against being overheard.

"I thought I might give Courtney Hood a ring. Make a trade. My future services for his present help."

"Not a bad idea. Besides, he's likely to keep an ear to the ground. He might know what's going on."

"Right." Alex went to the telephone and dialed Mr. Hood's number. After the usual interval, longer in Bangkok than in France or the United States, Lisette heard him say, "Hello. Mr. Hood, please. This is Alex Paul speaking.

"Oh, I see. Yes. Yes, give Mr. Hood a message, please. Ask him to call me back at this number, and tell him it's rather urgent—in fact, very urgent. I'll stay right here until I hear from him."

Hanging up, Alex said, "That was Miss Chieng Mai. She says her boss left the house early this morning, but she's expecting him back at any time."

143

"How good of you to tell her you'd wait," mocked Kyle.

Alex grinned. "I thought it was rather a nice touch."

"How are the pictures, Papaul?" Lisette asked. "Did they turn out well?"

"I haven't made prints yet, but the negatives look OK."

Kyle turned away to go to her desk. "At least," she said in passing, "we can still use the telephone."

When her father went back to his improvised darkroom, Lisette walked to the front door and looked down the paved roadway toward the gates leading to the Outside. Mr. Thanoo was not in sight. Probably he knew that the Americans would not be going anywhere this afternoon. In fact, a preternatural quiet had settled over the former quarters of the king's wives. Not a voice could be heard. No bird sang from the trees. Scarcely a leaf moved.

Overhead the sky itself seemed angry. Fat thunderheads looked like burned marshmallows, and a distant rumbling signaled the coming of the afternoon storm.

Today the downpour was torrential. The rain fell in a continuous curtain, shutting out the view beyond the villa steps. Lisette finished typing the work laid out for the day, then went up to her room and stretched out on the bed. She wasn't in the least sleepy, but she wanted to think.

She needed time to try to sort out her feelings about Bobby's terrible death, brought about by his own recklessness. She wondered where they had taken the body, who would notify his parents, and how they would manage the burial in this steaming tropical city halfway across the world from his home.

She wondered also where Don Hall was now. He had been marched away with the hippies as if he were one of their number. And was he? That was another question worth pondering.

He had not been with the first wave of campers marching on the tower. Of that she was sure. He had appeared later, just a moment before—or a moment after?—Bobby fell.

What had he been doing in the meantime? In those few crucial minutes, when even the guard from the temple was staring up in horrified fascination at the tower, where had he been?

X

The king is coming!

At first the news was a whisper on the lips of Mr. Thanoo, who hurried to the villa kitchen to inform the cook. Then the whisper swelled and spread, reaching the Thai servant girl and, through her, Lisette.

Lisette raced off to tell her father and pounded

147

on the darkroom door. "The king is coming, Papaul!"

She dashed upstairs again and called to Kyle, who was in the bathtub, "They say the king is coming. I wonder why?"

There were no special ceremonies scheduled at the palace, so far as the Americans knew. The Emerald Buddha would wear his rainy-season clothing for at least another two months, and no arrival of foreign dignitaries had been forecast by the English-language newspaper. Yet the king was coming! Lisette felt sure that his unscheduled visit must be directly concerned with this morning's events.

Her father and Kyle were inclined to agree with her. As the rain streamed down, turning the street into a shallow lake, they continued to speculate on the mysterious message sounded by the great bronze gong. "I give up. I'm going to stop guessing," Kyle said finally. "Besides, I have a feeling that we'll find out soon enough."

No telephone call had come from Courtney Hood during the afternoon, so Alex phoned again just before dinner. "He hasn't returned." Miss Chieng Mai sounded worried. "I can't imagine why."

Time dragged. Dinner seemed less appetizing than usual, and Lisette merely played with her food. Afterward, in the salon, Kyle and Alex started a game of chess, but neither became absorbed by the problems

148

of their knights or queens. The king—the real king—was the one who occupied their thoughts.

About ten o'clock Alex picked up the telephone again. The line was dead. "Well, that blows my chances for a news story," he said with a sigh.

Kyle looked worried. "There must be something very wrong indeed," she said after a while.

Lisette, more excited than apprehensive, walked to the open door and looked out at the liquid night. Near the gate to the Outside a light shone faintly, and there was a sound like a latch clicking. She waited, listening to a sloshing noise that seemed to be made by feet coming closer. Then gradually she discerned the familiar form of Mr. Thanoo. He was huddled under an enormous umbrella and complained audibly as he approached the villa. Only when he reached the steps did he resume his habitual poise.

Lisette moved back from the doorway. "Mr. Thanoo is here," she said.

Kyle, who was gathering up the chessmen, greeted the old man politely. "*Sawat dee*, Mr. Thanoo."

"*Sawat dee*," growled Alex. He was still annoyed at having found the telephone line dead.

Mr. Thanoo closed his umbrella and leaned it against the side of the house, just outside the door, then stepped across the threshold. He bowed ever so slightly, having dropped his former obsequiousness as if it were a cast-off disguise.

He spoke to Kyle in careful Thai, and Lisette, listening intently, caught two phrases—*proong nee,* which meant tomorrow, and *tam ruad,* police. Then he extracted a white envelope from under his shirt front, where he had been keeping it dry, and handed it to Alex, as though such an important missive should be delivered only to a man.

"Thank you," said Alex rather ungraciously. Kyle translated quickly. *"Kob koon."*

His business finished, Mr. Thanoo departed without waiting for Alex to open the envelope. Obviously he expected no message in return.

"I gather we're being summoned," said Kyle, as the guard disappeared into the night. "At least the police are to escort us somewhere tomorrow morning."

"Maybe the king wants to see us!" Lisette couldn't help exclaiming. "Wouldn't that be fun?"

"Oh, for Pete's sake, Liz!" Alex, who considered all royalty overrated, shot her a withering glance. "A king is no different from any other man." Opening the sealed envelope as he spoke, Alex drew out a folded sheet of heavy white paper bearing an impressive seal. Lisette and Kyle both came close to look over his shoulder while he read the message aloud.

Couched in perfect English, the note was short and to the point. Professor Goodfellow, Mr. Alexander

Paul, and Miss Lisette Paul were required to appear tomorrow morning at nine o'clock, at an audience hall near the king's private apartments. They were requested to be prompt.

A police escort arrived at the villa half an hour before the appointed time. Alex dressed for the occasion in jacket and tie, while both Lisette and Kyle wore simple summer dresses with short sleeves. Looking exceedingly dignified and proper, they set forth three abreast. Not even Alex felt like joking this morning; the appointment they were about to keep did not make for levity.

Lisette almost trotted in order to keep up with Kyle's long-legged strides. She had been awake since dawn, and her sense of excitement had mounted with the rising sun. She felt very alert, yet as if she were walking in a dream, because nothing about the fantastic Siamese buildings they passed was connected with her real life.

The policeman led them toward Dusit Hall, just behind the king's disrobing pavilion, a little gem that had once been reproduced to adorn an international fair. Guards, very erect and important, stood at the doors. As Lisette walked between them she felt rather intimidated and made a conscious effort to keep her eyes straight ahead.

Inside, she needed several seconds to adjust her vision to the dimness of the vast audience chamber with a throne of mother-of-pearl surmounted by a traditional nine-tiered white canopy. The throne was as disappointingly empty as the room.

Walking smartly ahead, the escorting policeman went to a door at the right and rapped, then pushed it open and stood back so the Americans could pass through. They entered a smaller room, with a long table behind which three men were seated. One wore a lightweight Western business suit. The other two were in uniform.

The men took no notice of the new arrivals. They were concerned instead with the group of boys standing in front of the table in a ragged line. Lisette searched for Don and found him second from the far end, looking as disheveled as the rest.

Three chairs were stationed near the center of the room well behind the campers, and Kyle and the Pauls were led toward them. The policeman indicated they were to be seated, then clicked his heels together and left.

The man in the business suit was addressing the boys in flawless English. "The question you still have not answered is why the young man you refer to as Bobby was persuaded to climb the spire of a sacred *prachadee*," he said with more than a trace of impatience. "You may reply in order, and you *must* reply. I'll repeat the simple question. Why?" He looked at the first boy in line.

"He just did it for kicks," muttered the fellow, as he scratched his arm nervously.

"For kicks?"

"For fun, like."

The examiner eyed the boy grimly. "I cannot believe that such a sacrilegious act would have been attempted for fun. Next!"

The black in Indian pajamas rubbed one bare foot against the other. "Bobby was kind of crazy."

"I didn't ask you for an opinion of your friend's mental stability. I asked why he climbed the spire."

"I don't know," the boy muttered. To Lisette, he sounded both frightened and sincere.

"Next."

A boy whom Lisette did not recognize kept sullenly silent until a companion kicked him in the shin. "Say something, can't you?"

"Bobby was on drugs. Sometimes he got wild ideas. Maybe this was one of them."

"Didn't you try to restrain him?" asked the examiner.

"You couldn't restrain Bobby. No way!"

"In fact, you actually applauded the performance, didn't you?"

153

"What's the harm in that?"

The examiner greeted the counter question with utter contempt. "Next," he said peremptorily.

The next three in line gave answers no more satisfying than those of their cohorts. Finally the examiner reached Don Hall, who seemed—at least to Lisette—more cooperative than the rest.

"I think somebody put Bobby up to the prank, sir."

For the first time the examiner looked hopeful. "And why do you think that?"

"Because it wasn't thought up on the spur of the moment. As these coves can tell you, he started planning the caper the night before."

The examiner's eyes flicked down the row of disreputable young men. "Is this true?"

There was a shuffling of feet, a grunt or two of assent, a muttered, "So what of it?" Nobody seemed pleased by Don's disclosure, yet nobody denied it.

"What's your name?" asked the investigator, looking back at Don.

"Don Hall, sir."

"Don, I want you to think carefully. Have you any idea—any idea at all—who might have instigated such a foolhardy performance?"

"No, sir," replied Don without hesitating.

The questioner tried another tack. "Suppose you tell us in detail how you learned of the plan." His voice had become softer, almost cajoling.

Don stood very straight, his hands clasped behind his back, the knuckles showing white, so that he looked to Lisette like a schoolboy hauled up before the principal. "It was sometime around sunset when I passed Bobby's tent on my way home from the city. He was talking to his gang, and I heard him say, 'Come on, dare me!' Then he called me over and asked if I'd like to get in on some fun. He even named a time the next morning and started passing out entrance tickets to all the kids who were willing to go with him to the palace grounds." Don paused, then said, "Those tickets cost money, sir. And Bobby was broke."

"How do you know that?"

"Because he wanted to move on to Iran—to Meshed—and he didn't have the funds to get there."

The interrogator's eyes swept the line of faces again, then settled on the boy standing next to Don, the only one he had not yet questioned. "Did this young man called Bobby promise to pay you if you accompanied him to the palace?"

The boy looked down at his feet. "Not exactly."

"What do you mean by that?"

"Well, he sort of held out the bait, like. He said if we went along he'd see we were taken care of."

The examiner returned to Don. "One more question. Have you any acquaintances in Bangkok?"

"A few, sir."

"Name them."

"Well, Mr. Courtney Hood. He's a friend of my father's. And I've met people at his house, his secretary and some of his clients and personal friends." He swung around slightly to indicate the newcomers. "Like these folks here."

All three men at the table seemed taken aback. Their attention shifted from the uneasy boys to the rear of the room, where Lisette heard her father groan softly. She tried to imitate Kyle, who was sitting very still and whose face was quite expressionless, but she felt her eyes blinking rapidly and realized that she was clasping and unclasping her hands.

After a few more questions, which elicited nothing, the boys were dismissed under guard. They straggled away sullenly, only Don managing to keep his head held high.

Immediately the interrogator turned to the three seated people. "Please be good enough to pull your chairs a little closer. Now tell me what you know of yesterday's unfortunate incident." He added pointedly, "I understand from the temple guard you were all on the scene."

Alex deferred to Kyle. "Professor Goodfellow—"

"As I assume you know, I am doing research for a book on the Grand Palace," said Kyle carefully. "I had gone to the *bot*—the Temple—to check on the absence of perspective in some of the murals depicting the life of the Lord Buddha, especially the one inside the entrance doors. Almost immediately after I arrived I was aware of a disturbance outside, a great deal of shouting and cheering. I followed the guard around the corner of the Temple to see what was going on." She paused. "You know the rest."

"You followed the guard? You mean he left his post?"

Too late Kyle appeared to realize that her statement incriminated the poor man, who would certainly be accused of negligence. "The chapel was empty," she said. "All the tourists were outside, watching the boy climb the *prang*."

"Thank you, Professor Goodfellow." The examiner turned to Alex. "Mr. Paul, where were you when all this was going on?"

"On a pagoda balcony." Alex described the exact spot in a manner that made Lisette listen to him with pride. He had dropped his slang and spoke like a man of culture. "I was trying to get a human-interest shot for our book, using the spires as a background, when the boys arrived." Meticulously he explained, "I wanted people in the picture, but not those particular people. So I gave up the shot."

Not a word about the Nikon, Lisette thought to herself. Alex was telling the truth, but not the whole truth, perhaps because he did not consider his news pictures had a bearing on the case in hand.

"Did you remain on the balcony, Mr. Paul, while the boy climbed the *prang?*"

"Yes," Alex replied easily. "But after he fell, I ran down to see if I could find a doctor in the crowd."

"And you discovered a doctor?"

"Yes. A German physician as it happened. Unfortunately, nothing could be done. The young man was already dead."

"And afterward?"

"We were required to get in line with the rest of the tourists, then sent back to our villa under the equivalent of house arrest."

A thin smile played over the examiner's mouth, but he didn't deny the statement. "How do you happen to know Mr. Hood?" he asked.

Alex hesitated only briefly. "Mr. Hood is an art dealer who is known to many Westerners interested in Thai art."

"I thought he dealt primarily in Khmer pieces."

"Perhaps." Alex shrugged. "I'm not an art collector. I'm a photographer."

"To go back to my original question. How do you *personally* happen to know Mr. Hood?"

"He looked us up and invited us to dinner one evening. He wants me to photograph his art collection, as a matter of fact."

Suddenly the examiner turned to Kyle. "Professor Goodfellow, were you acquainted with Courtney Hood before Mr. Paul's arrival?"

"Yes."

"Have you known him long?"

"Only by reputation. He sells to some private collectors and also to some art museums in the United States."

"When did you actually meet him?"

"Shortly after I arrived in Bangkok."

"Less than a month ago?"

"Right," said Kyle crisply.

"Thank you, Professor Goodfellow, Mr. Paul." The interrogator consulted some papers. "Miss Lisette, concerning yesterday's tragic accident, do you confirm what your father has told us?"

"Yes, I do."

"And have you anything to add that may have been overlooked?"

Hoping that she didn't look as guilty as she felt, Lisette shook her head.

The interview seemed to be over, yet the Americans were not dismissed. Their interrogator sat back in his black teakwood chair and said, "You may have heard that the king is in residence. That is true. Later on he may wish to speak to you personally, but in the meantime there are several things of which you must be informed."

159

Again he consulted a paper on the table before him. "First, the palace grounds have been closed to all outsiders until further notice. Only the young men detained in custody and those persons who normally live inside the walls will remain here. That will include your house servants, the caretakers who have accommodations in various buildings—and yourselves.

"Second, although you may walk in the grounds at will you must touch nothing. Nothing!" he repeated sternly. "Everything must remain precisely as it was yesterday morning. Do you understand?"

Alex nodded, Kyle said, "Quite," and Lisette whispered, "Yes, sir."

"Nothing must be moved, nothing altered, nothing touched. Special investigators who may wish to question you further will be at work. You will please cooperate with them fully. This is the king's personal request."

Again the Americans indicated that they understood.

"A third point. You may not leave the palace complex, nor may you communicate with anyone outside. As you perhaps have noticed, your telephone has been disconnected."

"May I ask, sir, what all these precautions are about?" Alex spoke with a certain asperity, triggered by the mention of the dead phone.

The examiner looked him in the eye. "You may, and I think it is time you are told. We are faced with a situation of the gravest importance, one that must be kept secret from the Thai people and the press at all costs."

After a trenchant pause, he said slowly and distinctly, "The Emerald Buddha has disappeared."

XI

Kyle recovered first. "But it's impossible!" she cried.

"One would think so, but it is all too true," the examiner said. "The Buddha vanished at the very moment the young man called Bobby fell to his death, after having desecrated the abode of God."

"You think, sir, that its disappearance is supernatural?"

163

"I try not to think, Professor Goodfellow. I am here to investigate all possible *natural* causes, and any help you can give us will be appreciated."

"Of course."

Crossing the sun-drenched courtyards on her way back to the villa, Lisette walked a little apart from her father and Kyle. She felt no personal reverence for the jade Buddha, yet her Catholic upbringing made her realize that to religious Thai people he occupied a place equivalent to the Virgin Mary. He was the sacred image revered above all others in the land.

Lisette also had learned, on her day's outing with Don, that the Thai people were very superstitious. Next to modern houses with television aerials on their rooftops she had seen little structures of wood or stone called "spirit houses," decorated with garlands, food offerings, and lamps lighted to propitiate the spirits who guarded the larger dwellings. Bangkok was a contradiction, with its high-rise buildings and its 381 Buddhist *wats*. The mood was modern, but ancient beliefs were still very strong.

Back at the villa, Lisette followed her father and Kyle straight through to the garden, where some chairs were placed in the shade of a banyan tree. The earth was still damp and steaming from last night's rain, but the heat of late morning couldn't penetrate the leafy canopy.

"What's so special about the Emerald Buddha?"

Alex asked irritably, as he settled himself on the end of his spine and stretched his legs. "If *I* wanted to make off with something, I'd hack a piece off that forty-two-ton solid-gold Buddha. It would be far more valuable than a hunk of jade."

"That depends on your point of view," said Kyle. "I seem to remember that Montezuma considered a gift of two pieces of jade to Cortés equal in value to two cartloads of gold."

"Gold was cheap in those days," muttered Alex.

"Besides," said Kyle, as if she hadn't heard the remark, "you have to realize that the Emerald Buddha is said to have special powers. The people believe that as long as it remains in this country, the independence of their homeland is assured. Its loss could be catastrophic. If the disappearance is leaked to the press, anything could happen—even war."

"Why say *disappearance?* Why not *theft?*"

Kyle looked thoughtful. "Very well, Alex. You like to play guessing games. Who could have stolen it, and how?"

For the first time Lisette spoke. "Even if somebody managed to get it down from its throne, how could it have been taken outside the palace walls? The alarm was raised almost immediately."

Kyle glanced at Lisette approvingly. "I think you've made a good point. I also think the Buddha is still somewhere inside."

"Hidden?" Alex asked.

"Obviously," said Kyle.

"Well, in that case the police should soon find it, and we'll have nothing to worry about."

"I should imagine," suggested Kyle, "that the police have been searching the buildings and grounds for the past twenty-four hours."

"With no success," murmured Lisette.

"What are you two doing?" Alex asked with a chuckle. "Plotting a whodunit?"

Kyle shook her head. "This isn't fiction. This is a *real* mystery."

Lisette, fearing they were getting off the subject, came back to Kyle's first question. "Who could have stolen it?"

"We don't know, but we do know that the hippies were probably hired to deflect the attention of the guards and the tourists for a few important minutes."

"Not *the* hippies—*one* hippie," put in Lisette, almost defensively.

"And that's a dead end," Alex quipped.

"Papaul! You shouldn't make a joke about that poor boy."

"I didn't mean to, Liz, honestly. It just slipped out."

Ignoring the interchange, Kyle said, "I keep wondering about Courtney Hood. What do we know about him, really? Except that he's rich."

166

"And that he's a fairly reputable art dealer," Alex said.

"How reputable? That's what I'm wondering," Kyle answered, while Lisette sat listening quietly. "Do you remember the conversation at the dinner party when the Englishwoman twitted Mr. Hood about his conscience?"

"He didn't seem to be very upset," Alex recalled, "and that Cambodian certainly defended him."

"A little too heartily, I thought." Kyle leaned back and lifted her long hair off her neck with both hands. She twisted it in a casual roll and anchored it to the top of her head with a tortoiseshell barrette in one graceful movement, while Lisette watched admiringly. She wished that she were light-haired and tall rather than slight and dark.

Then she happened to glance at her father and saw that he also was appreciative of Kyle's unstudied grace. Today she looked less than ever like a professor, yet the next moment she got to her feet and said, "Let's not waste the whole morning! We've got work to do."

While her father went off to his darkroom Lisette sat down at the typewriter. She didn't consider the morning wasted, far from it! Intense excitement was making her head spin, and her curiosity was mounting with every passing hour. As Kyle had indicated, they were all involved in a mystery that was very real.

As it happened, the notes to be typed today concerned the Emerald Buddha's astonishing history, which seemed to reinforce the claims to its supernatural powers.

Kyle had unearthed half a dozen versions of the Buddha's origin. One account suggested that it had been carved by a Greek sculptor from a big piece of emerald-green jasper mined in India, then enshrined in a temple in Ceylon until it was taken to Burma and began its peregrinations about the Far East.

Another chronicle read like a fairy tale. The writer claimed that a huge emerald had been carved by celestial beings in seven days and seven nights, then brought down from heaven by the king of the angels, who caused a golden palace to appear for the Buddha's resting place.

"Men who during their lives paid worship to him had their wishes granted," typed Lisette. The Buddha could bring happiness and survive disaster. Its special magic seemed powerful indeed!

The image had first turned up in Thailand in the fifteenth century, when an ancient pagoda in a northern province was struck by lightning, revealing a stucco Buddha partly covered with gold leaf. Not until a piece of plaster fell away did the priests discover the jade inside.

Now Lisette felt Kyle was getting down to facts.

The reigning king was brought to see the Buddha and was so delighted with it that he decided to move it to his capital, but the elephant carrying the treasure refused to take the road leading to the city. This refusal was taken as a sign of supernatural significance, and facts were again lost in a mist of conjecture.

Lisette paused to correct a spelling error and wiped her damp hands on some cleansing tissue. Typing in this climate had its problems. Everything was sticky, the paper as well as her skin.

What did the king do? Have the elephant beaten into submission? Not at all. He allowed him to take the road he had chosen and had the Buddha installed in a temple in a small town. Not until more than thirty years later did it reach the new capital.

Detail piled on detail; Kyle had done her research thoroughly. After a while Lisette became bored and started to yawn. She hoped the Buddha's travels were over, but apparently they had only begun. The temple in which the image was housed was repeatedly struck by lightning (another manipulation by the gods?), so the jade statue was moved to a neighboring province where it would be safe. Here it remained peacefully for a great many years, until a Laotian prince took it to help quell a rebellion. Apparently its power was now generally acknowledged to be very great.

169

On and on went the account. This same prince fled to Vientiane to escape Burmese invaders and carried the Buddha along. Not until 200 years later was it finally brought back to Thailand by King Rama I. Eventually it was installed in the Chapel Royal, "which is," finished the account, "its final resting place."

Final?

As Lisette typed the word she wondered if it was conceivable that the Emerald Buddha had been spirited off on still another trip. Once it was said to have traveled by boat accompanied by eight priests. At another time, a single priest had supposedly carried it the length of the country without detection. Everywhere the Buddha went the people prospered, and throughout all of its vicissitudes it had escaped harm.

No wonder the Thais thought the image magical. No wonder the present king considered its disappearance a disaster of national consequence. It was the one and only, the absolutely unique Emerald Buddha. Who would dare to attempt to steal such a renowned miracle worker? Not a Thai certainly! Lisette doubted that there was a Thai alive who would court the retribution that might be his after such a theft.

If not a Thai, then a foreigner. The question was, what foreigner?

And where was the Buddha now? Lisette was far too French to take stock in a supernatural disappearance. No flight of angels had carried that heavy piece of jade up over the palace walls.

As a matter of fact, she agreed with Kyle that the Buddha must still be inside the compound. The alarm had been sounded too quickly for any possibility of thieves escaping through one of the gates.

And every place had been searched. Every place! Even the big, clumsy wheelchair of the crippled monk. The lengths to which the guards had gone were almost absurd.

If I were a detective, Lisette thought, I'd long since have ruled out all possibility of the Buddha having left the grounds.

Very well. The theft had misfired in some way, but how? Lisette was dogged by a dozen questions for which she had no answers. Suddenly she wished she could talk to Don Hall.

It wasn't until late afternoon, when the daily shower had come and gone, that Lisette had an opportunity to take a solitary stroll through the courtyards that had once buzzed with activity. Although police were in evidence everywhere, the king's order that nothing be touched was being followed zealously. The souvenir stands were filled with fading postcards and sorry trinkets, the soft-drink cases were stacked untouched, one on top of another. Everything remained just as it had been at the moment when Bobby took his fatal plunge.

There wasn't a camper in sight. Have the boys been freed? Lisette wondered. Somehow she doubted it, because they were the only possible clue to the Buddha's disappearance. One of them might be holding something back.

Could it be Don? Lisette didn't want to suspect that Don knew more than he had told the examiner, yet she was aware that she knew the young Australian only slightly and that her trust in him might be misplaced. Don knew Mr. Hood. Mr. Hood knew Mr. and Mrs. Dillon. Now there was a likely suspect —the acquisitive Texas millionaire. Except that he hadn't been anywhere around on the fateful morning, and besides Lisette couldn't imagine him as a common criminal.

She could, however, imagine him yearning to own the Buddha! She could imagine him working through Mr. Hood, who might have hired thugs to engineer the actual theft, although the stakes would have to be huge indeed for any dealer to risk his reputation— perhaps even his life—with such a ploy.

Millions might be involved!

Mr. Dillon had millions, how many Lisette couldn't guess. Yet she was not impressed by either his appearance or his conduct. Perhaps Mr. Dillon was a cheat and a swindler who had achieved a spurious respectability.

Still thinking about the Texan, whom she had disliked when she first met him in Karachi, Lisette moved toward a building that sparkled as if studded with a thousand jewels. Actually the plaster facade was inlaid with bits of broken porcelain, carried to Siam from China in the eighteenth century as ballast on a ship and salvaged for the clever decorators. Although seen to the greatest advantage when distance lent enchantment, a closer view always amused Lisette. She stopped and ran a finger over a few of the colorful shards. At once a policeman appeared at her elbow, waggling a cautionary finger.

"Do not touch," he said in English. "Not touch anything."

"I forgot," Lisette apologized, although the restriction seemed silly. Taking advantage of the officer's knowledge of English, she asked, "Are the hippies still being held here?"

The man nodded.

"Do you think I could talk to one of them—Don Hall?"

The fellow looked doubtful. "I will ask," he said after a moment. "Come with me."

He led her back the way she had come, then disappeared into one of the newer Government buildings near the main gates. After an interval of perhaps ten minutes, he returned. On his heels came Don.

"Hi, Liz."

"Hello, Don. Are they still keeping you locked up?"

The boy nodded. "I hoped maybe you'd managed to get me sprung."

"Sprung?"

"Let out. Released." Don managed a wry grin.

Lisette shook her head. "I'm lucky to be allowed to talk to you." She moved a couple of steps away from the policeman, but the man followed, apparently determined not to miss a word he could understand.

"Don," Lisette asked, "where is Spooky?"

"Back at camp, I hope, keeping an eye on our things," replied Don promptly. "We weren't mixed up in this caper, you know. We wouldn't go along with a crazy deal like that."

"Yet you were there," Lisette said.

"Yeah, I followed along later. I was scared Bobby would get into trouble."

"And he certainly did." Lisette sighed. "Don, did Bobby ever meet Mr. Hood?"

Don's eyes widened. "Not that I know of. How could he?"

"I don't know," Lisette admitted. "I just wondered. How well does your father know Mr. Hood? Have you any idea?"

"Well enough, I should think. Mr. Hood used to live in Melbourne. I believe—way back then—he and my dad belonged to the same club." Don ran his fingers through his shaggy hair. He looked puzzled. "Hey, what is this? The third degree?"

At that moment a Thai official in a uniform heavy with gold braid came hurrying toward them. He nodded curtly to Lisette but addressed Don. "You are wanted by the chief examiner," he said. "At once."

"What's up now?" Don wondered aloud, and to Lisette's surprise he received a reply.

"I believe you are to be questioned concerning a missing Englishman."

XII

"Liz!"

As Don went off with his escort, Alex came striding across the courtyard, looking as angry as a baited bull. "Wasn't that Don Hall you were talking to?"

"Yes."

"I don't want you mixed up with that youngster,

do you understand? Just stay away from him from now on!"

Alex was acting so out of character that Lisette burst out laughing. "Don's only a semihippie," she said with unusual spirit. "He's a nice boy. I like him. Besides, Papaul, you told me yourself I could use a little shaking up."

"Look here! I'm responsible for you this summer, and—"

"*Tiens!*" Lisette interrupted. "*Tu es en colère.* You're acting like a parent at last!"

Alex was so taken aback he didn't finish his sentence. He stood looking both outraged and perplexed until Lisette, with a very French gesture of affection, took his arm and turned him toward the Inside. "Papaul, I've learned something that may be important. Mr. Hood apparently is missing. Remember, you couldn't reach him on the day the Buddha disappeared?"

Alex gave a long, low whistle. "Now the fat's in the fire for sure. We're bound to be called up for questioning again, and if we're connected in any way with the Buddha escapade, we may be forbidden to go ahead with this book."

The book, the book, the book! All Kyle and her father could think of was the book. Lisette was growing impatient with such grown-up preoccupation,

178

particularly when her own thoughts were completely taken up by a mystery that had engaged even the attention of the king.

Although she had once seen the president of France passing by in a motorcade, Lisette had never seen a real king, and she kept hoping that the monarch himself would appear at the next interview. But the same board of examiners sat at the long table, two military officers and the gentleman in the business suit whom Lisette thought of privately as Mr. No-name.

The flanking men again sat as mute as uniformed dummies in a window of the *Printemps* department store. Mr. No-name was the one who stated, with little ceremony, "Mr. Courtney Hood seems to have vanished into thin air."

Forewarned by Lisette that this news would probably be the reason for the meeting, Alex and Kyle greeted the information with polite interest but little surprise. Nobody spoke.

The examiner consulted one of his several papers. "He was last seen by his secretary when he left home at eight thirty on the morning of July 12, apparently en route to his art gallery in downtown Bangkok. He never arrived there. His car is missing, and Mr. Hood himself has not been heard from since."

"How very strange," murmured Kyle.

179

Alex appeared thoughtful. "I seem to remember an American to whom the same thing happened. He left his house one day and simply dropped out of sight."

Mr. No-name twitched his shoulders irritably. "Mr. Jim Thompson's strange disappearance caused our government great distress," he said with grave formality. "I can assure you the incident was most uncommon in a country as peaceful as ours."

"Peaceful? A tear-gas bomb thrown over the wall of a private garden is scarcely peaceful," suggested Alex. "Surely you must have heard of the incident at Mr. Hood's home from young Don Hall."

The examiner made no comment. Apparently he wished to pursue another line of attack. "I should like you to tell me what you know of the guests attending the dinner. Suppose we take them one by one. Professor Goodfellow?"

Kyle's orderly mind easily recalled what she knew of the Englishwoman and the Cambodian who had been at the party. She also mentioned Don Hall and Miss Chieng Mai.

"Was there anything in the least unusual about the conversation that took place?"

Shrugging ever so slightly, Kyle hesitated. "We talked about art, mostly. Cambodian art. Mr. Hood imports some rather wonderful Khmer sculptures, you know."

Mr. No-name nodded. "Think carefully, Professor Goodfellow. Can you remember precisely what was said?"

"Nothing out of the ordinary," replied Kyle. "The usual shoptalk of curators and collectors, except that during dinner the conversation turned to the subject of conscience and the legality of buying and selling artifacts out of the country of origin."

"And what was Mr. Hood's stand on this subject?"

Again Kyle hesitated and framed her reply carefully. "He believes that the rescue of any important piece of art is important, that the end, in other words, justifies the means."

"I see." The examiner turned to Alex. "Have you anything to add to Professor Goodfellow's statement?"

"Nothing," said Alex with a flickering grin in Kyle's direction. "She has covered the ground admirably."

"And you, Miss Lisette?"

Lisette could tell that the questioning glance was a mere formality, yet there was something she felt she should say. Ever since the mention of Jim Thompson, she had been thinking about the deep, dark canals and the finality with which a man could disappear. "I think you should know that I saw the Cambodian who was a guest at the dinner party again."

The examiner was mildly interested. "You did? Where?"

"At a house on one of the *khlongs*. A couple of mornings later Don Hall took me sightseeing." She ignored her father's groan at the mere mention of the boy's name and said, "We were in a boat at the floating market, and there was a traffic jam."

"Yes?"

"We pulled up near a private house built on piles, and while our boatman was tinkering with the engine, I heard two men arguing. Of course, I couldn't understand what they were saying, but suddenly I heard the name Courtney Hood. Then I recognized the Cambodian."

"How could you be sure?"

"Well, he's rather taller than most Thais and has a large mole on one cheek."

"Could you find the house again?"

"No. But I think I might recognize it if I saw it," Lisette said.

"Would Don Hall remember its location?"

"I'm not sure," Lisette confessed. "He wasn't paying much attention, because he was bargaining for a monkey."

Alex groaned again, audibly.

Mr. No-name, meanwhile, leaned close to the man on his right and held a brief, whispered conversation.

Then he straightened and said, "I think we shall test your powers of observation, Miss Lisette. We will fetch the boy and send you once more over the route usually taken by excursion boats."

"Look here," said Alex sharply, "I'd like to go along!"

"There will be no need, Mr. Paul. I can assure you that your daughter will be well chaperoned."

This promise was an understatement. Lisette was accompanied to an official car by two policemen dressed in the clothes of ordinary Thai tourists and a doe-eyed, smooth-haired woman in a long cotton skirt and collarless, buttoned jacket, who had apparently been requisitioned from the king's retinue.

She took her job as chaperone seriously and was as attentive as a duenna, listening to every word spoken by either of her young charges. Lisette couldn't tell how much English the woman understood. Not that it mattered really, because she and Don had nothing very private to talk about.

She was glad to be outside the palace walls once more. Even a luxurious prison, Lisette thought, is a prison nevertheless. The car, siren screaming, sped through the city with spectacular ease and brought the passengers quickly to the Oriental Hotel dock. There a small, swift motor launch was waiting to receive them, and the party was whisked across to the far side of the river and the channel to the *khlongs* foreigners usually visited. Today, however, the hour was later and most of the market people had sold their wares and returned home. Only a few sampans plied the water, and the scene was so different that Lisette found it almost unrecognizable.

On the morning that now seemed surprisingly long ago, they had chugged along at a snail's pace. Today the launch sped like a bird dog on a scent. "I'm completely lost," Lisette whispered to Don, whose eyes were bright and alert. "I don't recognize a single thing!"

"Neither do I," Don confessed. "This is a wild-goose chase, I'm afraid."

"I wish we could go slower," Lisette said unhappily.

Don turned to one of the plainclothes policemen. "Can we slow down a bit, please?"

The request was transmitted in Thai to the man at the tiller, and the launch was eased along at a more reasonable speed. The motor purred, the wake subsided, and Lisette breathed a sigh of relief.

"Don't look for the house," she advised Don. "Look for the place where the man tried to sell you the monkey." Suddenly she grabbed her companion's arm. "*Ooo-la-la!* Isn't that the same monkey? See! Over there!"

"It's not only the same monkey, it's the same man." Don turned to kneel on the seat and hail a fellow poling a slender sampan near the far shore. Then he turned to Lisette. "Get the boatman to pull over there. Maybe this bloke can help us."

"If he does," Lisette retorted, "you'll have to buy that gibbon." Nevertheless, she spoke quickly to the nearer policeman, and he in turn shouted instructions to the man at the tiller, who backwatered and turned the launch toward the little craft Lisette indicated.

"Sawat dee!" Don shouted the usual Thai greeting. Then he enlisted the help of an interpreter.

Yes, the man with the monkey remembered the young Australian. He held the furry creature out hopefully and started to jabber about a possible price. Don shook his head and the plainclothesman apparently asked if the gibbon's owner remembered the exact part of the *khlong* where the previous bartering had taken place.

The fellow thought for a minute or two, looking doubtful. His interest was only in selling the monkey. Growing impatient, Don asked Lisette, "Do you have any paper money with you? All I have in my pocket are a few small coins."

Lisette searched in her purse and pulled out the equivalent of a couple of dollars. "Will this be enough?"

"I should think so." Don showed the policeman the money. "Not for the monkey," he said firmly, "but for guiding us to the place where we met before."

The policeman explained to the man in the sampan, and the *bahts* proved an effectual bribe. Following the light boat as it shot through the black water, the sleek launch looked like a mackerel chasing a minnow.

The *khlong* curved to the right, then to the left. Lisette sat on the starboard side, scanning the near bank closely. Suddenly she stiffened. "There!"

At the same moment the sampan turned about and slid close to the launch's side. The monkey's owner pointed, Lisette nodded, the money changed hands, and the launch pulled up to the dock fronting the wooden platform that led to the house where Lisette had seen the Cambodian.

There was a quick interchange between the two policemen and the man at the tiller, not a word of which either Lisette or Don could understand. The plainclothesmen leaped ashore and ran quickly along an overgrown path, disappearing around the corner of the building.

The monkey's owner considered this a golden opportunity to pursue his sale. He stayed close to the launch, one hand holding the chain attached to the gibbon's homemade collar. As he chattered away in Thai, Don made brushing motions with one hand, trying to get him to give up and go away.

The chaperone, meanwhile, was sitting near the stern, quietly watchful. The launch's captain, distinguished by a visored cap, had one hand resting idly on the tiller. With the other he was lighting a cigarette. Far upstream two boys were playing like porpoises in the murky water, their shouts high-pitched and indistinct.

Lisette was scanning the house anxiously. It looked deserted today, the shutters latched, the door closed. Yet she had no doubt it was the place she had been looking for. Her sense of direction was poor, but her visual memory was very good indeed.

A woman with a straw hat shaped like a lamp-shade poled her boatful of salad greens downstream, passing the launch swiftly. Two birds alighted on the wooden platform, searching for crumbs. Don took Lisette's hand, and the chaperone stirred crossly. Time seemed to stand still.

The chaperone coughed. Don smiled gently, patted Lisette's hand, and moved slightly away from her. The policemen seemed to have been gone for hours, yet the captain's cigarette was only half burned down.

Lisette could endure the tension no longer. "The house looks empty," she said.

At that moment the porch door burst open. Two dark-skinned men, one short, one tall, both barefoot and dressed in singlets and cotton pants, came racing over the wooden planks as if demons were chasing them. They must have seen the launch, but they didn't hesitate for a fraction of a second, diving into the black water with the desperation of men in fear of their lives.

A shot rang out and a bullet whizzed over Lisette's head, puncturing the launch's canopy. Don suddenly caught her around the waist and pulled her down between decks, pushing her head low and shielding her body with his own.

There was another shot, off the bow this time, and a sound of flailing water. Lisette's breath came in short, apprehensive jerks. More running feet. A volley of shots. Lisette tried to raise her head to see what was happening, but Don growled, "Keep still!"

Out of the corner of her eye Lisette could see a bundle of Thai cotton on the floorboards near the stern. Her chaperone, duty forgotten, huddled like a heap of laundry, whimpering and keening by turns.

The firing stopped as suddenly as it had begun, and Don sat back on his heels, peering over the boat's rail. Lisette scrambled to her knees in time to see the younger of the two policemen pull up at the edge of the dock. He was looking toward a tangled patch of

188

bushes and trees on the opposite shore with the frustration of a man who had been thwarted.

The captain looked down at his scorched fingers and threw the stub of his cigarette overboard. He asked the policeman a quick question, but the officer shook his head.

"No sense trying to follow," Don said, as if he understood. "That's a jungle over there."

The Thai chaperone still crouched at the stern, holding her head in her arms. When the policeman spoke to her, however, she unrolled and settled back on a seat, smoothing her rumpled skirt with one hand while she wiped her eyes with the other, managing to smear kohl all over her cheeks.

Lisette glanced briefly in the woman's direction, then forgot her. "Those were the men!" Lisette called to the officer on the dock.

"Are you quite sure, Miss Paul?"

"Quite sure."

"Liz, you're dreaming!" Don objected. "These men had shaven heads."

"So they did, miss."

"So they did," repeated Lisette slowly. "But they were the men all right."

"Anyway," said the policeman, whose gun still dangled from his hand, "we've got one of them."

"What do you mean?" Don shouted.

The fellow jerked his head toward the house, the door of which was still standing open. "Inside," he said, "there was one that couldn't get away. He was trussed up like a guinea fowl."

Excitement made Lisette quiver. "What does he look like?" she called above the hubbub of a crowd that had begun to gather at the sound of the pistol shots.

The policeman pulled one of his ears and answered with care. "He's a foreigner, that's certain. Appears to be an Englishman."

XIII

"Mr. Hood!" breathed Lisette and Don simultaneously.

If they had found Courtney Hood, the escape of the two Cambodians seemed relatively unimportant! Lisette, anxious to verify their assumption, asked, "May we see him?"

The officer shook his head, looking very positive.

Don tried another approach. "Is the Englishman fair-haired?"

The policeman didn't answer. His attention was caught by a siren wailing in the distance. As it came steadily closer, he said, "We must go back to the hotel landing, where the car is waiting to meet us. My colleague will stay with the prisoner." He glanced from the young people toward the house, then said, "I will return in five minutes."

Fifteen minutes later he climbed aboard the launch and settled down next to the chaperone, who was still visibly shaken. Taking his gun from its holster, he laid it across his knees and kept a wary eye on either shore.

"If the Englishman is blond, we may know who he is," Lisette wheedled, as the boat sped back toward the river. "We'll tell you if you'll tell us."

The policeman, however, refused to talk. Evidently he had been cautioned by his senior officer to be quiet concerning the captive. Maintaining a dutiful silence, he continued his watchfulness.

Lisette and Don, however, were free to speculate. They spent the rest of the trip whispering together, careful not to lean too close, for fear of being reprimanded by the nervous chaperone.

"If Mr. Hood was tied up in that house, the Cambodians must be his enemies," Don reasoned.

"Unless it's a ruse."

"You've been looking at too much television," Don chided. "Plots within plots seldom happen in real life."

"We have no television at the manoir," said Lisette so primly that Don looked amused.

"I forget you're more French than American."

Lisette fell silent. She was trying to decide how far she could trust Don. Her thoughts flew back to their first meeting in the Temple of the Emerald Buddha, when he had mentioned the movie *Topkapi* and had wondered, aloud, how a couple of chaps might manage to steal the jade statue. How long ago that day seemed!

Yet how well did she know him now? In spite of her father's misgivings, she was sure he was not a member of Bobby's gang. He had faced the examiners openly and had tried to be helpful. She could not help believing in his honesty.

"Liz, there's something I ought to tell you," said Don, as the silence lengthened.

"Yes?"

"The palace police have let the rest of the fellows go."

"Oh!" Lisette's eyes clouded. Could she be wrong about Don after all?

His candid grin reassured her. "They've really checked me out," he said. "Even phoned my pop and one of my teachers in Melbourne to make sure I was a right guy. Then they moved me to a decent room and gave me the news about the Buddha. Swore me to secrecy and all that, but said they had to hold me because of my connection with Mr. Hood."

Lisette breathed a sigh of relief. "Don, can you keep another secret?"

"Unless the cops decide to torture me. If they start to pull out my fingernails one by one, I will tell all."

Lisette shuddered. "Don't even joke about such things." She was remembering the ancient punishments for stealing or defacing a sacred image. "I'm pretty sure," she confided, "that those two Cambodians were on the scene when the Emerald Buddha disappeared."

"You saw them?"

"I think so. There were two monks in yellow robes. One was pushing the other in a huge, outlandish wheelchair that looked like a converted *samlar*. The tall one, who seemed to be crippled, had a mole on his left cheek."

"Hmph." Don didn't sound particularly impressed.

"So did the Cambodian at Mr. Hood's dinner party," Lisette reminded him with quiet emphasis.

"Heck, lots of people have moles. I have one myself, on my right shoulder blade."

Lisette brushed the remark aside. "Why would

they shave their heads and come to the palace in disguise?" she questioned. "At that particular hour, on that particular day?"

"It does seem strange," Don admitted.

"I remember seeing them near the Temple, then again at the main gate, when all the tourists were searched."

"Were they searched too?"

Lisette nodded.

"Then they didn't get away with anything."

"Certainly not with the Emerald Buddha," Lisette agreed.

The launch turned back into the river and sped past the Temple of Dawn, which looked like a gargantuan wedding cake resting on a grassy bank. Almost too quickly, Lisette found herself at the dock, where she and Don were hurried back to the car and driven to the palace.

"Who knows when and if I'll see you again?" said Don sadly, as they rolled through the carefully guarded gate.

"I suspect it will be soon," Lisette returned. She blew him an impish kiss as her chaperone led her toward the villa.

"Take care!" called Don.

"You too."

Once home, Lisette looked for her father, but the

villa seemed to be empty. At this time of day Kyle was often somewhere on the grounds, and Alex was usually in his darkroom. Wanting to report on her adventure, Lisette knocked on the closed door.

"Give me three minutes!" her father called.

She waited impatiently, although Alex was usually as good as his word. When his time clock rang off, he opened the door instantly, switching on an overhead light.

"Come in, Liz. I'm glad you're home. Any luck?"

"All kinds," Lisette told him. "Cops and robbers, shooting, and best of all I think we've found Mr. Hood."

"You're kidding!" Alex sank down on a chair facing a table cluttered with the paraphernalia of his profession. There were stacked boxes of film, strips of negatives, a few finished color photographs. From a line strung from a light fixture to a nail near the door a couple of sheets of Nikon prints hung swaying. Lisette's entrance caused them to move slightly in the air.

Quickly she told her father the story of the expedition, emphasizing the fact that they could not be absolutely sure the Englishman was Courtney Hood, but that it sounded very likely indeed.

Alex seemed troubled. "You mean to say the policeman fired shots at the Cambodians?" he asked.

Lisette nodded. "Right over our heads!"

Pushing back his chair angrily, Alex said, "I won't have it! I won't put up with such nonsense. You could have been killed!"

"I'm perfectly safe, Papaul," said Lisette soothingly.

"You were to point out a house, not get involved in a gun battle!" Alex got to his feet abruptly. "I'm going to see the king!"

"Papaul, please!"

Even as Lisette spoke Alex slammed the door behind him, creating enough of a draft to disengage a sheet of prints from the clip by which it was attached to the line. Automatically Lisette went over to pick the sheet up, then dusted it off and ran her eye along the series of snapshots her father had taken while Bobby climbed the spire.

There he was, surrounded by his cheering cohorts, scrambling up the two-tiered base. Like a puppy carrying a bone, he was clutching the flag between his teeth. Next he was starting the ascent as the crowd of spectators grew. Alex had caught a shot of the tourists turning back from the model of the Angkor Wat, and another of the two painters, standing open-mouthed beside their vat half full of whitewash, with cans of paint forgotten in their hands. The camera moved in again on Bobby, partway up the *prang,* climbing—Lisette realized—toward his death. Alex was shooting faster than ever. Bobby three quarters of the way up. Bobby nearing the top. Bobby taking the cord from his pocket. Then another shot of the swelling crowd and the frantic Temple guard.

The boy falling, like a puppet tumbling through the bright air. Captured on film, Lisette saw the action during which she had covered her eyes. The sequence ended abruptly with a final shot of the body on the ground. At this point her father had stripped off his camera and hurried off to see if he could help.

A shattering few minutes, linked inextricably to the disappearance of the jade Buddha. But how?

Lisette studied the sheet of prints again and discovered a significant omission. Although there were four shots of the watching crowd, in not one of them could she find the pair of Cambodians masquerading as monks. There was no picture of the clumsy wheelchair, no shaven heads, no yellow robes. Perhaps her father had missed them by sheer chance. Perhaps they were on the outskirts of the throng, out of camera range. Yet their absence was cause for thought.

At this point Alex burst into the darkroom, his determination to see the king apparently deferred. "It *was* Courtney Hood!" he announced explosively. "I just saw him walking by with a couple of detectives. Right past this very door!"

"Did you speak to him, Papaul?"

Alex shook his head. "They wouldn't let me."

"What a shame." Lisette's brain was simmering with a dozen questions she'd like to ask Mr. Hood, although she doubted she'd get satisfactory answers. If he was innocent of any connection with the crime, he wouldn't know; if guilty, he wouldn't tell.

In any event, she was glad Mr. Hood was alive and presumably unhurt, that he hadn't met a painful end in the Bangkok of subtle undertones, mysterious deals, and political intrigue. This second Bangkok terrified Lisette, because it was in such violent contrast to the city of cheerful, open, friendly people.

"How much do you bet we're called on the carpet again?" Alex was saying, when Kyle came into the darkroom, her wide brown eyes sparkling.

"You've been wanting to see the king, Liz. Well, you're going to have a chance."

"When?" Lisette clapped her hands excitedly.

Alex growled, "Good! It'll save me the trouble of looking him up."

"What are you talking about?" Kyle demanded.

"Papaul's all upset about some shooting," Lisette replied quickly. "Nothing really happened. Nobody was hurt."

"Plenty happened!" her father contradicted. He told Kyle about the gunplay involved in the escape of the two Cambodians and the rescue of Courtney

Hood. "Imagine involving this child in such a fracas! I'm going to complain to the king himself!"

Lisette burst out laughing. "Papaul, please! First you want me to be more grown up. Then you treat me as if I still wore pinafores."

"Stand up for your rights, Liz," said Kyle with a throaty chuckle. "Your daughter is sixteen years old, Alex, and a very competent sixteen, I might add."

Pleased but embarrassed by the compliment, Lisette backtracked to the beginning of the conversation. "When are we going to see the king?"

"At six o'clock this evening," Kyle replied. "It isn't an audience or any sort of social occasion. He simply wants to talk to us."

"What did I tell you?" muttered Alex. "More questions."

"I wonder," asked Lisette, "if Mr. Hood will be there?"

"I'd think it likely," said Kyle, then glanced at her watch and excused herself to take a shower and change her clothes.

Lisette, anxious to look her very best, washed her hair and toweled it dry, then put on her favorite dress. Imagine meeting the king! I must write to Philippe and Maman and tell them all about it, she thought, as she stood before her bedroom mirror regarding her image critically.

Somehow this simple frock seemed scarcely the right attire in which to walk into a royal presence. She wished she could have looked like Anna, in yards and yards of lawn and ribbons, and she pictured the king as a replica of Yul Brynner, younger perhaps, but dressed in the exotic clothing of a Far Eastern potentate. Not until Kyle reminded her that he was apt to be very Western, and that he was a gifted amateur jazz saxaphonist, did she try unsuccessfully to revise her expectations and visualize a ruler in more conventional dress.

Alex had put on a white shirt and jacket for the occasion. Lisette suspected that he had even trimmed his beard. Kyle looked at him approvingly when they met in the salon to await their police escort. "Pretty sharp," she said.

Alex flushed. "You're looking pretty sharp yourself." He turned to Lisette. "Wouldn't you say Professor Goodfellow has a certain pizazz?"

Lisette was faintly shocked. "Papaul, what a thing to say! Kyle is an intellectual."

"An attractive girl and an intellectual aren't mutually exclusive, my dear. At this particular time in history women are *supposed* to have brains."

Kyle laughed and murmured, "Alex, behave," just as the escort marched up to the door. Lisette glanced at her father, who said, "Ready, set, go!" and they went off at once toward the Inside gates, which were standing open to let them through.

As she walked across the familiar courtyards Lisette was aware, more than ever before, of the emptiness of the palace grounds. The whole place had a sepulchral quality, as though the disappearance of the Emerald Buddha were like a death.

Where was the little god? Where *could* he be?

If a corps of detectives, a battalion of special investigators, couldn't come up with an answer, how could she?

Yet Lisette had a strange premonition that she knew something they didn't know or something they hadn't discovered. Absurd, she tried to convince herself, yet the feeling persisted. Somewhere, buried in the reaches of her subconscious, was a clue that she had failed to recognize, something important that nobody else had seen.

"Liz, stop daydreaming. Come along now," Alex urged.

Lisette dogtrotted a few paces to catch up with her father and Kyle, who were rounding the corner of the Temple of the Emerald Buddha where the painters' abandoned cart, its vat full of scummy whitewash, still blocked a direct path to the common entrance door.

"Are we going *here*?"

"Apparently."

The door stood open; the interior was lighted. A man in civilian clothes came across the copper-tiled floor to greet the Americans. They immediately recognized the grave-faced examiner who had interviewed them twice before.

The police escort remained outside the door, and in the chapel the silence was intense. Stockinged feet made no sound as the trio moved forward, so Mr. No-name's conventional "Good evening" seemed to rumble and reverberate.

He paused for a moment for emphasis, then said, "In a departure from custom, you have been brought to this most sacred of all temples in order that you may see with your own eyes the empty throne of the most precious of Thailand's Buddha images."

Nobody spoke. All eyes lifted to the high altar, past the glittering demon guardians made faintly absurd by the vacant seat above.

"His Majesty, the King," continued the examiner, "wishes you to be reminded once more of the seriousness of the Buddha's disappearance. Should the country discover its loss, havoc would ensue. Students might be incited to riot, priests to violent demonstrations, and the military could even seize the opportunity to revolt."

He paused again, then said slowly and resolutely,

"The Emerald Buddha must be found and returned to its historic resting place."

Lisette looked up at the golden throne, almost expecting the Buddha to materialize, but the space it had occupied was still shockingly bare. No miracle occurred.

Nor did the king appear. From the chapel the trio was led to the royal apartments, inside which not even Kyle had set foot. They were taken through an anteroom to a chamber where portraits of past rulers looked down from the walls and two equerries stood at attention just inside the double doors.

The ceiling was high, the furniture elegant but sparse, and to Lisette the place seemed as empty as the chapel—as empty and as ominous. The examiner bowed and departed, disappearing behind a tall carved screen at the far end of the room and leaving them to decide whether to stand or sit in the un-comfortable-looking chairs arranged along the walls.

Alex tried to make a joke, but it fell flat. Neither Lisette nor Kyle even smiled. Actually Lisette scarcely listened to what her father was saying. She was won-dering why Courtney Hood wasn't here. Then her speculations came to a abrupt halt. The moment she had awaited was at hand.

From behind the screen another equerry appeared, to announce in ringing tones that echoed in the vast hall, "His Majesty, the King!"

XIV

Lisette's first reaction was one of intense disappointment.

She hadn't expected Yul Brynner on a white elephant—well, not exactly—but she *had* hoped for royal robes. Instead, the man who entered the room wore an ordinary sack suit, and aside from a diamond tiepin he looked disconcertingly conventional.

On second glance, however, Lisette had to acknowledge that he was more handsome than the film star. Slender, with a pointed chin but an astonishingly square jaw, the king was light-skinned for a Thai and had black, curly hair that was glossy and neatly groomed. He walked toward his waiting guests quickly, shook hands with all three in a casual, Western manner, and got immediately to the point.

"I have asked you to come here because I am forced to deliver an ultimatum," he said in perfect English. "Since, regrettably, the Emerald Buddha has not been found, we have decided to make the palace grounds forbidden territory once more and must ask you to abandon the project on which you are working. Arrangements will be made for you to leave the country by Garuda Airlines tomorrow night, and I shall count on your discretion in not mentioning the tragedy here."

Kyle looked stricken. Alex was obviously indignant. Lisette, who knew how much the book meant to them, could scarcely stifle a gasp. With the work less than half finished, they were to be penalized for the loss of the Buddha, even though they had nothing whatever to do with the affair.

Alex was the first to recover. "Your Majesty, the book can be completed within a fortnight, if—"

The king cut him off. "I sincerely regret your disappointment, Mr. Paul, but the decision is final, unless, of course," he added with a gentle smile, "the Buddha should reappear."

"May I ask a question or two, Your Majesty?" Kyle spoke easily and unhurriedly, yet Lisette could sense her tension.

"Of course."

"May I ask what your investigators have learned from Mr. Courtney Hood?"

"Mr. Hood apparently was kidnapped by two armed men disguised as mendicants, who intercepted his car on a little-traveled road leading from his home to the highway. He recognized one of them, a Cambodian with whom he had been engaged in a questionable business deal. To be explicit, he claims the Cambodian offered to sell him some fragments taken from the site of the Angkor Wat."

Looking directly at Kyle, the king said, "You are aware, Professor Goodfellow, that the Angkor Wat is as precious to the Cambodian people as the Temple of the Emerald Buddha is to the Thais."

Kyle nodded. She seemed shocked.

"The Cambodians quite rightly resent such sub-rosa negotiations," the king continued. "My ministers suggest that Mr. Hood's illegal dealings have so angered our friends across the border that they were driven to take violent steps in retaliation."

Lisette, listening carefully, assumed he was referring to the kidnapping.

"They also suggest that Mr. Hood's erstwhile Cambodian contact was attempting to discover just how far Mr. Hood was prepared to go. When he learned that the art dealer was even willing to countenance the robbing of the Angkor Wat, he threatened him in a number of ways in an attempt to bring him to his senses."

Remembering the tear-gas bomb, Lisette wondered what the other ploys had been.

"Threats were to no avail, so they kidnapped him? Is it as simple as that?" Kyle asked.

The king nodded.

"Excuse me, Your Majesty!" Lisette spoke breathlessly, overcoming her shyness because she had something important to say. "The two Cambodian men disguised as monks were here on the morning the Emerald Buddha was stolen."

An indulgent expression in the king's eyes changed to interest. "You are quite sure of that?"

"Positive," Lisette replied. "I got a good look at them when they came running out of the house on the *khlong*. Except, when they were here at the palace, the tall man with the mole on his cheek was in a wheelchair, pretending to be crippled."

"I saw them myself," Kyle remarked thoughtfully. "They were ahead of me in line at the main gate."

Lisette wasn't finished. "The strange thing is that

when everybody—*everybody,* even the guard—was watching Bobby climb the spire, the monks weren't anywhere around."

"There was quite a big crowd, Lisette dear," said Kyle. "You may have missed them."

"I'm absolutely certain they weren't there, Your Majesty," Lisette persisted. "My father took pictures of the entire happening and they don't appear anywhere on the prints."

"Pictures? I thought all film was confiscated," the king said sharply, turning to Alex.

Too late, Lisette realized that she had revealed her father's deception. "Your Majesty, I had one roll," she confessed.

"You still have the prints, Mr. Paul?"

"Yes, Your Majesty."

"I should like to see them."

"Let me go get them, Papaul!" Lisette begged, to cover her confusion. "I know just where they are."

One of the equerries was detailed to escort her to the villa and back again, with the caution not to let her out of his sight. Lisette trotted along at the man's side like a scolded child, sorry for her indiscretion, yet convinced that the absence of the two spurious monks was significant. She got the prints quickly and studied them once more on the return walk. Then on the very threshold of the king's apartments, she stopped short and held the sheet up to see it more clearly in the light of a brilliant sunset painting the western sky.

"Mais, oui!" she cried suddenly, then turned in a flash and raced off toward the Temple.

The astonished equerry, shouting Thai appeals and imprecations, pounded along on her heels, but she didn't even glance back over her shoulder. Excitement filled her to bursting, while her feet sped over the pavement and up the steps to the Temple compound, ten yards ahead of the panting, outraged guard.

The chapel doors were closed and locked, but Lisette wasn't heading toward them. She stopped in front of the row of stone lions, close to the painters' cart with its brimming vat of whitewash. After consulting the sheet of prints for a final time, she flung both arms in the air and let out a very unladylike, very American shout of triumph. "Whoopee!"

If the indignant equerry had been a few feet closer, she would have hugged him. Instead, she called, "Hurry, hurry!" and was about to dart past him when she felt her arm grasped in a firm and rather painful grip.

Ignominiously she was marched back to the royal apartments by a flustered official who obviously thought she had gone mad. Shining eyes, skipping steps, and undignified shouts made no sense to him at all.

Lisette, however, was too elated to pay her escort any heed. The moment he released her arm she almost danced across the floor of the big salon, where the king was still standing with her father and Kyle.

She no longer cared that she wasn't dressed in crinolines like the captivating Anna, that she was slight and dark rather than tall and blond like Kyle. She held in her hand a secret, a big, important secret, one that she alone had guessed. Instead of being swept by stage fright in the presence of a monarch she felt like the heroine of a drama in the last exciting moments before the curtain was about to rise.

"Here are the snapshots, Your Majesty."

The king took the sheet from her hand, then looked curiously at Lisette, who couldn't conceal her jubilance. Her father and Kyle exchanged a puzzled glance, then stood quietly while the monarch ran his eye along the succession of contact prints.

"You're quite right," he said finally. "The two monks appear nowhere. This is a clue that deserves further investigation."

Such solemn adult reasoning didn't dampen Lisette's high spirits. "Please, Your Majesty, look at the pictures again. Do you see anything else out of the ordinary?"

For a second time the king studied the prints carefully. "Nothing."

Lisette's excitement had reached its peak. The curtain was up. She was on stage. "Your Majesty," she said with a triumphant smile, "with the help of my father's pictures I have found the Emerald Buddha!"

"Liz!"

"Child!"

Lisette turned to her father and Kyle with a joyous grin. "I haven't gone crazy. I know where it is! I'm positive I'm right. Come, I'll show you!"

The king hesitated, then gave a very slight shrug, subtly indicating his desperation. "Out of the mouths of babes—" he murmured to Alex and Kyle, then summoned the equerries and let Lisette walk beside him as she led the way to the Temple.

Once more she stopped short of the row of lions, right beside the painters' cart, and pointed to the huge vat filled to the top with scummy whitewash. "In there," she said.

The King signaled to two of his servitors, who stripped off their uniform jackets and plunged their arms into the viscous white emulsion. The expressions on their faces changed from controlled disgust to astonishment. Quite forgetting their discreet training, they shouted unintelligibly in Thai.

"It's there!" breathed Kyle, then unexpectedly took command.

"Don't let them attempt to lift it, Your Majesty. It might slip. First drain off most of the whitewash, then get a sling rigged up. I'll show them how, if you like. I've often been in charge of moving heavy pieces at the museum."

The king issued quick orders. Servitors ran for a siphon and an empty tub. Lisette felt her father's arm go around her shoulders, and she wriggled happily. "How did you guess?" he asked.

"I should have guessed sooner," Lisette told him. "One of your pictures, taken before the Buddha was stolen, shows the tub of whitewash half full. Afterward the vat was filled to the brim. Some heavy object must have been put in it—like the Buddha!"

"You're so right." Admiration colored every word Alex spoke. "And you're so smart, Liz! That was a great scene you played out with the king."

"Sh!" Lisette cautioned, but she needn't have been concerned that the king would overhear. He was still issuing orders, and within minutes new arrivals from the royal apartments hastened up the steps. By the time the Buddha emerged dripping from its milky bath, the audience had swelled to a throng.

Under Kyle's direction every precaution was taken, and the netted image, like a great fish being taken from the sea, was settled slowly on the deck of another sturdy cart.

A prolonged sigh of appreciation swept the spectators, a sound recognizable in any language. "A-a-h!" With the fading of the last of the sunset two servants lit torches, and in their light the king walked over and touched the Buddha's cheek. Then he wiped off his fingers and came over to Lisette.

"We are very grateful," he said simply, as he bent to kiss her hand.

XV

"To my darling daughter, who not only found the Buddha but who saved our book!" toasted Alex, as he raised a glass of the champagne the king had sent to the villa by special messenger.

His eyes moved from Lisette to Kyle, who looked beautiful in the candlelight. Her tanned skin was glowing and her eyes were very bright.

Don Hall made the fourth at the table. He had been fetched from his room at Lisette's request—the king and his staff would do anything to please her! —and was finding his first sip of champagne intriguing. "Tastes like a strange sort of ginger ale," he said.

Alex laughed and consulted the label on the bottle. "The king would not be amused. He has sent his very best."

Dinner was an hour later than usual. The food was ruined, but it didn't matter. Don had already eaten, and none of the others were hungry. They were still too excited and relieved to care what they ate or if they ate at all.

All over Thailand, from the northernmost province of Chiang Rai to the central plains of Phattalung and Yala Pattani in the south, Thai police were searching for two Cambodians with shaved heads. The king wanted them apprehended speedily, and what the king wanted he generally got.

Lisette tried not to think of the fugitives. She suspected that even contemporary Thais could, when the occasion warranted, be ruthless in their punishments. The others at the dinner table were still talking about the Buddha, which was soiled but safe.

"I suppose," said Kyle, toying with the stem of her champagne glass, "that the thieves hadn't counted on having to take the attached chunk of jadite projecting below the actual statue. That must have been a surprise!"

"I think the wheelchair gimmick was interesting," said Alex. "I suppose they planned to hide the statue under the monk's full robe."

"But the extra chunk of jadite made them change their plans," suggested Don.

"I agree," said Kyle with a quick nod. "If the Buddha proved, quite unexpectedly, to be too big to make off with in the wheelchair, the thieves were forced to abandon the statue at the last minute. And the big vat of whitewash, only half full, was standing right there!"

Conveniently in front of the Temple steps, Lisette mused. Out of sight from the side, where everyone was concentrating on Bobby inching up the *prang.*

"I wonder if they planned to come back later, scale the wall in the dead of night or something? What do you think, Alex?" Kyle inquired.

"I've stopped thinking." Alex grinned as he poured some more champagne. "Thinking and celebrating don't go together. I'd rather celebrate."

That it was indeed a time for celebration, everyone agreed. "It's like a reprieve," Kyle said with an almost tremulous sigh of relief.

Lisette knew she was thinking of the book. How discouraging it would have been to return to Boston empty-handed, with all her research wasted! Alex had even more reason to be delighted over the return of the Buddha. Anxious to show his gratitude, the king would now surely grant permission for the jacket photograph.

Alex raised his glass again. "Everything's coming up roses!"

"Papaul, be careful!" cautioned Lisette. "Maman says champagne can be intoxicating if you drink too much."

She was surprised when everyone laughed, but pleased when her father pushed back his chair and came around the table to stroke the top of her head. *"Plus ça change, plus c'est la même chose,"* he quoted in one of his rare attempts at French.

The maid brought coffee to the salon, and although it was late when the tray was taken away, Lisette couldn't bear the thought of going to bed. "Let's walk as far as the fountain, Don," she proposed, as her father and Kyle went out the glass doors into the garden.

Alex turned, glanced at his watch, and frowned as a matter of course. He still regarded Don with a certain disfavor.

Kyle burst out laughing. "Oh, for heaven's sake, Alex, come along," she said.

Stars crowded the summer sky, and a crescent moon hung like a golden brooch over the banyan tree.

The air had cooled with the approach of midnight, and temple bells tinkled in the distance, brushed by a breeze so faint that Lisette could scarcely feel it against her hair.

Don took her hand and led her to a bench near the fountain, which was playing gently, the water sparkling in the light of the moon. "It's been quite a day, hasn't it?"

Lisette nodded.

"I wish I could have been in on the climax. It would have been great to see the Buddha hauled up, dripping wet, like Venus rising from the sea."

Lisette smiled. "I wish you could have been there too. But whitewash doesn't look much like seawater."

"I wish your father liked me," said Don unexpectedly.

"Never mind." Lisette gave the boy's hand a comforting squeeze. "You have to *learn* to like people, Don." She was thinking of herself and how she had resisted liking Papaul. "Give him time."

"Time is running out." Don sighed. "I've got to go home."

"Back to the river, you mean?"

"Back to Melbourne."

"Oh, no! Not so soon! Why we're just getting to be good friends." Lisette looked as forlorn as she sounded.

"I'm glad you feel we're friends," said Don rather gruffly, "because I do too. Will you write to me, Liz, when I get back to school?"

"If you want me too."

"I do." He took a folded slip of paper from the pocket of his khakis. "I've got the address here," he said, as he handed it to Lisette. Then, with boyish fear of becoming too emotional, he changed the subject. "It'll be winter in Australia, you know."

Lisette sat staring down at the white square of paper without speaking. The moon burnished her hair, touched the ovals of her fingernails, and fell softly on her bare, brown legs. She was thinking about Philippe, to whom she owed a letter, and Brittany seemed to swim in the distance like a landscape in a dream. This was reality, here and now. How could she ever explain to Philippe that she had changed?

"Liz, don't be sad."

"I can't help it."

Clinging to a future reality, Don said, "You'll write to me when you go back to France?"

Lisette nodded. Yet she forced herself to face the probability that she would never see Don again. Australia was very far away from New York or Paris, and the years ahead would be crowded with a thousand new experiences nobody could foretell.

Suddenly she flung her arms around Don's neck and pressed her cheek against his. "This has been the best!" she whispered, then jumped up and ran for the villa, unable to say a proper good-bye.

The remaining weeks in Thailand passed swiftly for Kyle and Alex, who worked day and night on the book. Lisette wrote frequently to her mother, and once more to Philippe. *"Ce fut un été merveilleux,"* she told him. A fabulous summer indeed!

She was sorry when Don flew back to Australia, but she wasn't especially lonely. During the long afternoons she wrote in her diary, going back over the past days and carefully recounting the story of the Emerald Buddha's disappearance and recovery.

The two Cambodians were apprehended trying to cross the border at a little frequented point, and the story they told made their motives for the attempted crime more understandable. For years Cambodian officials had been trying to halt the surreptitious sale of Khmer art treasures to dealers in Thailand, but to no avail. Both sellers and buyers were greedy, and king among the buyers was Courtney Hood. He paid well and quickly, and he would apparently stop at nothing to acquire an artifact he could resell profitably to a wealthy customer like Mr. Dillon.

Mr. Hood ignored warnings. Threats appeared

useless. Finally, out of desperation, the Cambodians decided to try to implicate the ruthless dealer in the robbery of an art treasure precious to the Thais. If Cambodian agents could kidnap Courtney Hood, then steal the Emerald Buddha and arrange to have the sacred image found in his apparent possession in the house on the *khlong,* he would be implicated in the robbery. The end would be gratifying, because the Thai government would then take the action the Cambodians so heartily desired.

Of course, the plan went awry, but even so Lisette felt that the Cambodians had managed to accomplish their purpose. Although he had committed no real crime, Mr. Hood had been thoroughly discredited, and Kyle predicted he would be forced out of the business that had made him rich.

Actually Lisette saw Courtney Hood only once again, when he was marched past the villa by a guard. She learned later, however, that his beautiful house was up for sale and that his collection had been confiscated by the Thai Government and returned to Cambodia.

At the palace, the days resumed their normal calm and leisurely pace. For more than a week museum experts worked on the restoration of the Emerald Buddha and its rainy-season garments. The image, polished and gleaming, was returned to its high throne before the palace gates were again opened to the public, and Alex was invited to set up his Hasselblad in the chapel and take photographs of the venerated statue to his heart's content.

The king returned to his summer palace, but not before sending a splendid note of appreciation and a white jeweler's box to Lisette. It contained an intricately linked gold bracelet of beautiful Thai workmanship and an exquisite charm of clear green jade in the exact shape of the Buddha. When Lisette wrote a respectful note of thanks, she told the king she would treasure it for the rest of her life.

As time grew short the pace quickened. Alex developed the jacket shots of the Buddha and spread them out on a table so that they could choose among them. Kyle and Lisette at once settled on a resplendent, glittering picture that seemed to capture not only the quality of the image but the fantasy of the palace itself. "So be it," Alex said, and marked the back of the print with a lightly penciled star.

Later the same day Lisette came across her father stretched in one of the low chairs in the villa garden. She came up behind him noiselessly and glanced down over his shoulder at some layout sketches he was making with the jacket in mind. He had indicated the space to be taken up by the glossy photograph and had roughed in the lettering:

Text by Kyle Goodfellow
Photographs by Alexander Paul

As Lisette stood watching he erased the two lines and substituted another:

Text and Photographs by Kyle and Alexander Paul

Lisette gave a slight gasp, and he became aware of her presence, but didn't seem in the least embarrassed. As he looked up at her over his shoulder, he said, with a lopsided grin, "Just trying it on for size."

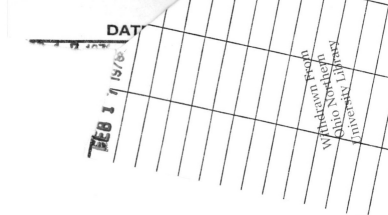